THE BALTIC CONVOY

The Baltic Convoy

SHOWELL STYLES

FABER & FABER
London and Boston

First published in 1979
by Faber and Faber Limited
3 Queen Square London WC1
Printed in Great Britain by
The Bowering Press, Plymouth and London
All rights reserved

British Library Cataloguing in Publication Data

Styles, Showell
The Baltic convoy.
I. Title
823'.9'1F   PR6037.T96B/

ISBN 0-571-11260-9

AUTHOR'S NOTE

This third and final sea adventure of
Lieutenant Michael Fitton is based on the
factual record in James's *Naval History* and
the Log of His Majesty's gun-brig *Cracker*.

ONE

Sea Lords

Old Martin, chief clerk in the Trade Division of the Admiralty, stood looking out of one window and sorrowing for the view from another. From his old office in the main Admiralty building he had been able to see all the comings and goings in Whitehall; seven years ago he had watched Nelson drive out through the gates on his way to Trafalgar (September 12th, declared Martin's phenomenal memory, was the date of that final visit) and seventeen weeks later to the day he had seen the little Admiral's coffin carried out to a waiting funeral car designed to look like his flagship. This present window, his since his transference to the newly-instituted Trade Division office a year ago, could command no such memorable scenes. It overlooked the cobbles of Craig's Court, a cul-de-sac opposite the Admiralty, and apart from the daily arrival and departure of the curricle driven by the Honourable John Stannard, head of Trade Division, the cobbles bore little traffic other than the tread of official messengers in blue coats with brass buttons.

Nevertheless, old Martin spent a good deal of time standing at the window of his office. It was a chief clerk's privilege, in his opinion. Moreover, a chief clerk's quill needed frequent reshaping, for which a good light was essential, and he was accustomed to have a pen-knife and a quill in his hands during these window-watching spells. On this early autumn afternoon, indeed, his excuse was less adequate, for he was engaged (or pretending to be engaged) in fitting a ready-cut quill to a wooden pen-holder, a newfangled device recently decreed by Their Lordships to be used in all Admiralty offices. Martin scowled distastefully at this innovation and wagged his grey head irritably. Nelson gone; the feathered-quill pen gone. This wasn't the way to beat Bonaparte.

"Bramah," he said suddenly, "Joseph. Four dozen Bramah locks delivered five-eleven-eleven. Three gross wooden pen-holders delivered eighteen-seven-twelve."

There was some satisfaction in accurately recalling the name of the Pimlico inventor and the dates of Admiralty transactions with him, but it was a poor use for a memory trained to retain matters more closely concerned with the struggle against Napoleon. In his old office on the other side of Whitehall his work had been among the files of warships and their commanders, and he had been used to claim—possibly with justice —that he could recollect at a moment's notice the service record of any officer who had held command. Now his retentive mind automatically registered details of dockyard consignments and similar humdrum matters.

He slid the quill finally onto the holder and was about to return to his desk when a sudden clatter of hooves and wheels brought him back to the window. A carriage had swung into Craig's Court—those were Admiral Duckworth's bays and that was the Admiral himself in the carriage; it was like Sir John to have himself driven across from the Admiralty when he could have walked the distance in five minutes. He could have no other purpose but to call on the head of Trade Division and Mr Stannard had better be warned—swiftly, since he was usually dozing at this hour. Martin trotted to the inner door and knocked loudly on it. After a pause of some seconds a sleepy voice bade him come in and be damned.

Martin opened the door and put his head into the room. "Admiral Duckworth's calling on us, sir—I hear him on the stair now."

"Deuce take him!" Stannard, a stout gentleman with a choleric eye, sat up and adjusted his neckcloth. "But Martin— see he's admitted instantly, and hold yourself ready to help me sit on him if necessary."

Rightly interpreting this latter order in a figurative sense, Martin returned into the outer office just as the door to the stairway was thrown open and the Admiral stalked in. Sir John Duckworth was lean and greyhaired, and his pale blue eyes sparkled as irascibly as Mr Stannard's for all that the whites were yellow-tinged from the fevers of the West Indies station. As Third Sea Lord he was responsible for the building and repair of His Majesty's ships of war, their guns, and their stores. His necessary liaison with Trade Division was an uneasy one, since he and Stannard heartily disliked one another, and a personal visit such as this was certain indication of urgency and—almost as certainly—of complaint. To rebuff complaint and "sit on" Admiral Duckworth, the Honourable John might need the support of his chief clerk's departmental knowledge and remarkable memory.

"Servant, Sir John," said Stannard from the open doorway of his room.

The Admiral nodded stiffly and passed him without pausing in his stride. The door closed behind them. But Martin, deciding that his superior would hardly throw him out again when his presence could mean useful support, slipped in unobtrusively and glided shadow-like to a corner of the big room where the drawers of a filing bureau gave him an excuse to rummage and listen with his back turned to the speakers. The Admiral, seated opposite the head of Trade Division at the mahogany table, began without preamble.

"I've been absent for ten days, Mr Stannard, at Lord

Kennet's place in Sussex. I return to find chaos, absolute chaos." He banged his fist on the table. "And damned dangerous chaos, I may add."

"In what respect, Sir John?" demanded Stannard cautiously.

"In respect of masts and spars for His Majesty's vessels of war, sir! My room at the Admiralty is crammed, absolutely crammed, with demands for masts and spars."

"But surely the dockyards—"

"The demands, sir, are from the dockyards! Portsmouth, Chatham, Devonport, Sheerness—they haven't ten fathom of pine between 'em. I have eleven 74's refitting, sir, and three more have come in since yesterday. All require spars replaced, five require new masts." The Admiral stared accusingly across the table. "Where are they?"

"At a guess," said Stannard with half a grin, "they're alongside the quays at Boston or New York—and that's not my fault."

The Third Sea Lord, with a visible effort, controlled his rising temper. When he spoke, after a pause of several seconds, it was in a cold and level voice.

"Though I can hardly credit it, Mr Stannard, your levity suggests that you have not perceived the urgency of the situation. I explain, therefore, what you should be well aware of. You realise, I take it, that this nation stands alone against Bonaparte with all Europe on his side?"

To this sarcasm Mr Stannard replied by raising his eyebrows and shrugging his shoulders. Duckworth nodded and continued with a patience that was intended to exasperate.

"Wellington's eight fighting divisions in the Peninsula are all that stands between Bonaparte and world conquest. A small army to face the Emperor's millions, Mr Stannard, and it would not long survive if only one of Bonaparte's fleets broke out from the ports where the Navy holds them blockaded.

Toulon and Venice, Rochefort and Brest and Cherbourg, Antwerp and the Texel—we haven't ships enough to blockade them all and yet we are doing it. As for the Danish Baltic ports, one 74 and two frigates is the best that Admiral Saumarez can do there. I hope I don't need to point out that one ship-of-the-line sent home from the blockade for repairs must materially weaken it. And I have fourteen in for refit, Mr Stannard—fourteen—with not a spar for the dockyards to give them."

The Admiral's secondary purpose of annoying the head of Trade Division had given way, as he spoke, to his primary purpose of dealing with an urgent problem. His bony face showed real anxiety rather than ill-temper. Stannard, perhaps not unmoved by the blunt recapitulation of Britain's present dangers, refrained from a riposte.

"I admit all that, of course," he said briskly. "The cause of the shortage you complain of is, as you know, the failure of the American timber convoy. If the United States hadn't declared war on—when was it, Martin?"

"Eighteenth June, sir," said Martin instantly, looking up from his drawer.

"Yes. If that hadn't been the case the problem would not have arisen. And the timber contracts with the Americans—"

" 'Ifs' will not solve the problem, Mr Stannard," the Admiral broke in, recovering his acerbity. "Trade Division should have provided against such a shortage."

"I was about to observe, Sir John, that the American contracts were put in hand without reference to this department." Stannard leaned back complacently, assured now of putting his adversary on the defensive. "I was not officially informed of them. I had to assume that the dockyards were adequately supplied. I can't accept the blame for the inefficiency of some fellow on t'other side of Whitehall."

"There's no question of inefficiency there, sir!" Duckworth

said sharply. "The necessity of making unofficial arrangements with the American traders was forced on us by the Non-Intercourse Act. They were prepared to evade their President's law and supply us with timber, but it had to be done quietly. One of their largest convoys was on the point of sailing from Boston when President Madison's declaration of war was made known. I fancy you know this as well as I do, Mr Stannard."

Stannard eyed him askance. "I fancy I do, Sir John."

"And yet, God damn it, you did nothing about it!"

"I haven't said so."

The Admiral's lean cheeks reddened and he sucked in his breath audibly.

"It's evident, clearly evident, that you did nothing about it," he said impatiently. "Else there would not be this dearth of masts and spars. Sweden should have been approached the instant war with America became certain. The Swedes are our one remaining source of supply. Neutrals though they are, they have not so far refused their trade—"

"A moment, Sir John, if you please." Stannard turned to speak over his shoulder. "The date of the Stockholm order, Martin."

"Twelfth July, sir," replied the chief clerk without hesitation. "Eight shiploads, it amounted to. The *Cherub* sloop, Lieutenant Fisher in command, sailed from the Downs that day with the order."

"Eight shiploads of good pine timber for your masts and spars, Sir John," said Stannard, nodding at the Admiral with maddening benevolence. "I fancy that will remedy the dearth you speak of."

The Third Sea Lord looked as if he wished that the Honourable John held rank as lieutenant or post-captain; even a post-captain can be ruined by an Admiral's word.

"And why was I not informed of this?" he growled.

"Why, sir," Stannard said blandly, "it appeared to me that

you considered communication between our two offices unnecessary."

Duckworth glared at him but let it pass. "You tell me this order was dispatched on the 12th of July. We are now at the end of September. Why have these eight shiploads not reached the dockyards?"

"The fortunes of war, Sir John.—Martin!"

"Sir?" Obedient to a nod, the chief clerk came and stood at one side of the desk table.

"You transcribed Mr Fisher's report. Please to recall it for us—the gist, not the whole," Stannard added hastily; Martin, he remembered, was quite capable of repeating these things verbatim.

"Yes, sir." Martin cleared his throat. "On the 15th July the sloop *Cherub* was attacked by five Danish gunboats three miles north of the entrance to the Sound. In beating them off she received extensive damage to hull and spars and her rudder-post was shot away. Mr Fisher ran his vessel aground on a bank six miles south of Anholt island in order to effect the necessary repairs and it was not until the evening of the twenty-second that he was able to—"

"Very well, very well!" barked the Admiral. "I take it that *Cherub* did eventually complete her mission, that Stockholm agreed to supply eight shiploads of timber, that a convoy was arranged despite all this delay." He jabbed a forefinger at the Trade Division man. "I want to know when that convoy will arrive."

Stannard sat back and stared at the ceiling. "Let me see. The escort for the convoy—a gun-brig, Martin, I fancy?"

"Gun-brig *Cracker*, sir."

"Ah. Well, *Cracker* sailed for the Baltic, escorting two merchant vessels to Gothenburg, on—"

"Twenty-third September, sir," supplied Martin as he paused and snapped his fingers.

"Just so. *Cracker*, having seen her charges safely into port, will rendezvous with *Courageux* and receive her orders as to picking up the westbound convoy. It's possible she's doing so at this very moment—eh, Martin?"

"Quite possible, sir."

"So the eight shiploads, Sir John, should anchor in the Downs within the week," Stannard concluded.

"If," amended the Admiral with emphasis, "if they get through the Sound." He leaned forward with forefinger accusingly pointing. "You send a mere gun-brig to escort a convoy of eight ships—a most valuable convoy, on which, conceivably, may depend victory or final defeat in the present war. Was that the best you could do, Mr Stannard?"

"Yes, Sir John—it was," Stannard countered pugnaciously. "If you can find me a frigate that can be spared for a Baltic convoy, or even a second gun-brig, you'll do more than Admiral Louis could do. There are two frigates already in the Baltic—"

"*Clio* and *Hamadryad*," interpolated Martin beneath his breath.

"—but I'm told they can on no account leave their present station. I have no need of excuses, Sir John," added Stannard in a less aggressive tone. "What you yourself said a moment ago is only too true—we haven't ships enough."

For a little while the Admiral sat silent, drumming his fingers on the table. Then he got slowly to his feet.

"If I were a praying man," he said gravely, "I would pray that this convoy may come safe to port. You impressed on *Cracker's* commander the importance of his mission, I hope?"

Mr Stannard stood up. "Of course—a most courageous and reliable officer. We may count upon him."

The two gentlemen exchanged the brief civilities of parting and the Admiral, attended by Martin, went to the door. Here he paused and turned.

"You have heard the old tale of the campaign that was lost for lack of a horseshoe nail, Mr Stannard," he said in the same grave tone. "This Baltic convoy may be our horseshoe nail."

The door closed behind him. Mr Stannard, grinning, cut a few steps of a jig and flung himself into his chair. Then he frowned. Then he took a glass and a bottle of Madeira from the drawer where he had pushed them on the Admiral's arrival. He was sipping Madeira, still frowning, when the chief clerk re-entered the room.

"Well, Martin, we sat on him," said Stannard reflectively, "but that don't please me as much as it ought. I've been remiss—I admit it to you. I should have interviewed this gun-brig commander, as I told Duckworth I'd done. What sort of fellow is he, d'ye know? Young fire-eating lieutenant, I suppose."

"Lieutenant, sir, but if I'm correct—" Martin, for the first time that day, had to strain his memory—"past middle age, or nearly. I believe he was in Their Lordships' black books after some West Indies affair. On half-pay for four years before present appointment."

"Good—God!" Stannard gulped his wine and set the glass down empty. "Duckworth's right. We'd better betake ourselves to prayer. What's this poor devil's name?"

"Michael Fitton, sir," said Martin.

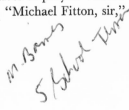

TWO

The Escort

I

Michael Fitton, seated at the table that occupied about a quarter of the deck space in his hutch of a cabin, penned an entry in his Log and waited for the ink to dry. *Anchored in 11 Fms. Anholt island NNW 27 miles. Light W'ly breeze & hazy.* It was likely, he thought, to be the last entry on that page, which was headed "Remarks at Sea 1st October 1812". *Cracker* would weigh for the twenty-mile run to the entrance of the Sound tomorrow, at two bells in the middle watch; if this quartering breeze held steady she should be through the dangerous part of the narrows—less than four miles of water separating Danish Elsinore from Swedish Helsingborg—before there was light enough for the Danish gunners to try long-shots at her. This would be the seventh time the gun-brig had passed the Sound and it was almost as familiar as the run in behind the Goodwins to the Downs. A faint smile crinkled Mr Fitton's square and usually impassive face as he recalled his first passage southward along that four-fathom channel into the Baltic, nerves at full stretch and the lead going all the time; the knowledge that he could safely keep close in to the Swedish shore, at or beyond the extreme range of the guns of the Kronenburg fort, had come later.

Familiarity, reflected Mr Fitton, who was of a philosophical turn of mind, should breed confidence, not contempt. Certainly it would not do to be contemptuous of Bonaparte's Danish allies. Deprived of their entire battle fleet in two successive battles, the Danes had yet managed to maintain their attack by using gunboats, large pulling-boats mounting a 6-pounder in their bows; not long ago a British sloop had been all but sunk by gunboats a mere two-hour sail from *Cracker*'s present anchorage, which was why he had stationed lookouts at bows and stern and cautioned Honeyburn, his second-in-command, to keep silence on deck. Gunboats approaching by night would reveal their presence by the sound of oars, since they often pulled ten oars a side. Once through the Sound and in the southern waters of the Baltic there should be little danger of enemy attack, for those waters were constantly patrolled by *Courageux* and her two frigates. It was from *Courageux* that he was to receive his orders concerning the westbound convoy, making rendezvous with the 74 off the island of Bornholm "on the 2nd October or not later than 5th October". The gun-brig had been delayed by headwinds in her passage to Gothenburg but she should sight Bornholm on the 3rd or 4th.

Mr Fitton put the Log in its rack on the bulkhead and stowed quill and ink-bottle in the drawer under the table. The cabin was in the stern below the quarterdeck and there had been just light enough from the small glazed port for his log-writing, but now the daylight was fading and the cabin was very dark. A clatter of feet on the ladder from the quarterdeck was followed by a knock on the door. Foden, one of the three ship's boys, came in with a lighted lantern, preceding a very short seaman carrying his commanding officer's supper on a tray. Foden hung the lantern on a hook in the low deckhead above the table and the seaman, christened Hezekiah Band but inevitably Shorty to his shipmates, offloaded his tray to the accompaniment of his usual commentary, which Mr Fitton had come to tolerate because it obviously gave Band much pleasure.

" 'Ere we are, sir, not such as we could wish to hoffer but good 'olesome vittles none the less—'ot pea-soup in this mug, sir, a nubbin of salt beef fresh as they come, the last of the Deal bread we took aboard five days ago—stalish it is but better than 'ard tack which we'll be on for the rest o' the cruise—and beer, sir. *And*—" Shorty's tone heralded a *bonne-bouche*—"a fine ripe slice of Swedish cheese, sir, bought by meself off the bumboat at Gothenburg."

"Very well, Band."

It was a solecism for a captain to say "thank you" to a lower-deck rating though he would use the phrase repeatedly, and almost meaninglessly, to his subordinates of commissioned or warrant rank. Mr Fitton took care that his expression showed his pleasure.

"I hope you recovered your money from Mr Grattan," he added.

Grattan the cook had charge of a fund subscribed by the upper deck.

"That I did, sir." Band was quite ready to expatiate further. "What's more, I 'ad the bumboat woman bringing down 'er price for some fish, 'andsome they was, too, kind o' sea trout, but Grattan, 'e says—"

"That'll do," said Mr Fitton briefly, taking up his spoon.

"Aye aye, sir."

Shorty turned and scuttled out with surprising quickness, pushing the boy before him, and *Cracker*'s captain was left to sup in solitary state.

Thirty-two years in the Navy and command in a series of little ships had convinced Mr Fitton that solitary state, a strict maintenance of aloofness, was of vital moment to any officer in command of a ship; especially to a middle-aged lieutenant who was nominally captain of a 12-gun brig with a crew of thirty-eight men and three boys. It had taken him eight months to achieve this in *Cracker* but he had done it, and the three floggings and one desertion that had taken place in that period were well below the average number for a gun-brig. Having established that he was just as powerful a monarch as the captain of a ship-of-the-line, and erected an impregnable barrier between himself and the rest of the ship's company, he was able on occasion to ignore the barrier—where everyone was at such close quarters he had often to do so—and retire behind it again with no weakening of discipline. In the result he had a happy ship, an orderly and efficient crew, and the solitude which he had always preferred to human society.

Michael Fitton was aware that he was well liked by his crew. He knew that there had been fierce competition for the privilege of acting as "captain's steward"—a privilege involving work additional to the ordinary duties of an able seaman—and that two black eyes and a cut lip had been Hezekiah Band's badge of office for the first day or two. It was typical of him that his popularity surprised him. Seeking a reason for it, he found it (as he thought) in a story current on the mess-deck for'ard that he was the dispossessed heir to an earldom, with the bluest of English aristocratic blood in his veins; a story he strongly suspected to have originated with his second-in-command. Mr Henry Honeyburn, if indeed he was responsible, had only elaborated a little on the truth, for Mr Fitton was the last (barring his ten-year-old son) of those Fittons of Gawsworth whose ancestor had stood with his peers to witness the signing of Magna Carta. And it was a curious fact that the British fighting seaman would far more willingly obey an order given by a "born gentleman" than one given by an officer who had worked his way up from the lower deck. The real cause, however, was that Mr Fitton was one of those rare leaders whom men will follow and die for no matter where they lead; in this alone he was like the arch-enemy Bonaparte. Despite his long record of successes in small-ship actions—or perhaps because official recognition of them had been so cruelly denied—he still did not realise his power. Nor would he have understood that it was exemplified by the fact that he finished the fine ripe slice of Swedish cheese although it was the sweet-tasting *getost* and repellent to his palate. He washed the taste from his mouth with the last of the beer, picked up his cocked hat from the cot, and went on deck.

Cracker lay easily to her anchor in a circle of darkening twilight, opaque yet faintly luminous. The Kattegat was in one of its calmer moods and the little dark waves that slapped at her hull scarcely lifted her in their ceaseless progress from bow to stern. Mr Fitton's first glance was upward to the squaresail yards of the two masts, just visible against the greyness overhead; he could make out fore and main courses, topsails, and topgallants loosely furled and gasketed, so his orders had been carried out. It was always advisable to check such matters when Mr Honeyburn was the executive. He turned to the tall, thin figure who had crossed the quarterdeck and was saluting him ceremoniously.

"Nothing to report, sir," said Mr Honeyburn. "The river glideth at his own sweet will—and there you have it."

"Thank you." A voice, briefly loud then swiftly stifled, came to his ear. "Go for'ard and stop that noise, Mr Honeyburn, if you please. I'll have the next man that speaks above a whisper flogged."

"Aye aye, sir. Extremely naughty of them."

Honeyburn stalked away along the narrow deck to where the watch squatted gossiping under the rail between two 18-pounder carronades. Mr Fitton lifted his square shoulders and let them fall; he was resigned to Mr Honeyburn by now, but still found him disconcerting.

Though a 12-gun brig was one of the least of naval commands she was required to carry two commissioned officers. Thus, when Lieutenant Fitton was appointed to her a year ago, he was at once presented with Lieutenant Henry Honeyburn, four years older than himself but junior to him by reason of the fact that his lieutenant's commission was dated six months later. How Honeyburn had ever succeeded in passing the examination for that commission was something to wonder about during uneventful night watches. He appeared to know little of seamanship and less of navigation, though he had somehow acquired a rather erratic knowledge of gunnery and ballistics and an enthusiasm for these arts which made his long, amiable, and somewhat vacuous face light up with unwonted intelligence whenever it was necessary to load a gun. According to his own account, he had been a schoolmaster until his readings in the poems of one William Wordsworth had fired him to exert himself in the cause of freedom. Somehow he had got himself into a midshipman's berth and there had been every chance that he would stay there, one of the thousands of middle-aged midshipmen who through drink or incapacity would never rise any higher; but by what could only have been a miracle—unless, as Mr Fitton sometimes tended to think, drink or incapacity had blinded his examiners —he had been commissioned lieutenant in 1804. Among his many failings was a disposition to sprinkle his conversation with tags from his favourite poet; among his merits were perfect good-humour and a sort of absent-minded indifference to danger or discomfort. Mr Fitton, whose reading was among dead philosophers rather than living poets, had come to tolerate the quotations from the works of Mr Wordsworth, which he found more amusing than irritating. As for the ex-schoolmaster's inefficiency in his role of *Cracker*'s first lieutenant, his senior had only to consider the various kinds of undesirables he might have got in his stead to accept Honeyburn's sobriety, even temper, and general amiability in lieu of sterner virtues.

The brief consideration of his odd subordinate had taken Mr Fitton across the gently-heaving deck to the after rail, where a dim and bulky shape leaned motionless in the gathering gloom.

"You know what you're listening for, Peters?" he said.

"Them bl—them Danes, sir," said the lookout. "Oars gruntling in th' rollocks."

"Very well." That was a word apt to the sound, that *gruntling*. "Report any sound you hear to Mr Honeyburn at once. Don't wait until you're certain it's oars."

"Aye aye, sir."

Mr Honeyburn, his mission for'ard completed, was performing his usual meticulous salute. He was absurdly punctilious in observing his brother lieutenant's seniority on all occasions, but Mr Fitton knew that the acknowledgement was offered in all sincerity; there was no sarcasm in Honeyburn's simple nature.

"I shall turn in now, Mr Honeyburn," he said. "No need to remind you that I'm to be called instantly if the approach of any vessel is suspected."

"Probably no need," agreed his first lieutenant reflectively, "but a wise reminder all the same. 'The soberness of reason—' "

"Good night," said Mr Fitton hurriedly, and went below.

Ten years ago, he thought as he descended the ladder, Honeyburn would have tried his patience sorely. Now his impatience had gone overside with his ambition and he was ready to tolerate all men and all things that did not explicitly oppose his duty as a sea officer. He had achieved at least the status of a philosopher although he could never, now, achieve those starry heights of post-captain and admiral—perhaps even a peerage, like Nelson—for which he had striven in the face of

26

repeated frustration. Down in the lamplit cabin he groped in his locker for the tattered book, once calf-bound but now held together with tarry cord, which had been his *vade mecum* for half a lifetime in the Navy. The words of Epictetus were familiar enough without looking them up in the *Moral Discourses* but it was a comfort to read them for the hundredth time: *True instruction is this—learning to will that things should happen as they do.* Yes, he had learnt that. Contentment was the true gold of life, ambition the false metal; a greater poet than Honeyburn's Mr Wordsworth had said, "By that sin fell the angels."

Mr Fitton took off his jacket and loosened his neckcloth, dowsed the cabin lamp, and lay down on his cot, which was fitted athwartships so that the gentle pitch of the gun-brig rocked him as in a cradle. The rhythmic groan and creak of the timbers, the fainter and more remote treble of the westerly in the rigging, made an accustomed lullaby too often repeated to be noticed. He could get three hours' sleep before he relieved Honeyburn and took the middle watch, which would be a busy one; up anchor at two bells and away south-east through the night to the entrance of the Sound. Usually he would have been asleep thirty seconds after putting his head down, but tonight his thoughts kept him awake for a good five minutes, pursuing the reflections started by that glance into the *Moral Discourses*. It was curious to recall by what devious paths he had reached contentment at the age of forty-six, an ageing lieutenant happy in the command of a small and unimportant ship, with no prospects but retirement on half-pay and final slow decay in Greenwich Hospital.

There had been the brave days of teenage as "captain's servant" and midshipman, when his mother had been alive and they had both believed that his brilliant naval career would end in the Fittons regaining their rightful place among the great families of England; the long years of deferred promotion and waning hope; the glitter and glory of the Caribbean adventures, when "very gallant conduct and superior professional abilities"—and the total of forty-two valuable prizes taken—had at last brought him his commission, ten years overdue; the bitter enmity of an admiral, which had kept him unemployed on half-pay for nearly four years; and at last re-employment in little ships, *Archer* in the Channel and *Cracker* on Baltic convoy duty. Those three decades of his past were remote as a blue horizon far astern. He could remember them without bitterness or regret—as he remembered Mary and the tiny cottage at Gawsworth.

Michael Fitton had married Mary Rushton in what might be called a reaction of despair, when he had been sent home after the Peace of Amiens and believed that the Navy would never employ him again. He knew he had never really loved his sharp-tongued wife but he had been loyal and affectionate and a good husband; their son Frederick, now ten years old, was being brought up by his grandparents. For Mary had died three years ago, and Mr Fitton, drowsy in his cot aboard *Cracker*, could not find any reproach for himself in his memory of her. His enduring love for ships and the sea had left him no room for the passionate love of a woman—and in any case, he told himself comfortably, he was too old for that sort of thing now. He shifted his head on the coarse pillow, sighed once, and was instantly asleep.

2

The westerly breeze had freshened at midnight and *Cracker* was snoring along through the darkness with the wind over her starboard quarter, her best point of sailing.

"How's her head, Mr Sholto?" asked Mr Fitton.

"Sou'-east, sir, dead on."

"Bring her a trifle closer. Steer sou'-east by east."

The gun-brig's deck tilted very slightly over to leeward as she brought the wind more on her beam.

"Course sou'-east by east, sir," reported Sholto.

That should offset the leeway she would have made in the last hour, reflected her commander. In his careful estimation his position was now some dozen miles west-nor'-west of the Kullen point on the Swedish side of the entrance to the Sound; with Sholto's sensitive handling *Cracker* should be able to run straight for the narrows, where—with ordinary luck—a light or two in sleeping Helsingborg would give him bearing and distance.

Only in a naval vessel as small as a gun-brig, and probably in few of those, would it be possible for a boatswain to be given a trick at the helm. Between *Cracker's* little hierarchy of two lieutenants and the lower orders for'ard there was the middle class of three warrant officers—cook, carpenter, and bos'n. Grattan, Trapp, and Sholto were all entitled to the honorific "Mister" and like all their kind were insistent upon their professional superiority to the manual labourers of the lower deck. But Mr Fitton had discovered that Sholto, the lean redheaded bos'n, was by far the best helmsman on board, having that special sympathy with the ways of a ship under sail which is inborn rather than acquired. For this blind passage of night sailing, by dead reckoning in shoaling waters, he needed Sholto's hands on the wheel-spokes to counteract the insidious tendency of the quartering wind to edge the brig off course, and it was a measure of the concord in his ship's company that Mr Sholto had taken his post as quartermaster without the least demur.

Mr Fitton went to the weather side of the little quarterdeck and stood gazing into the blankness of night ahead. No stars gleamed through the overcast, but the haze of yesterday evening had cleared for he could make out the moving wave-ridges a pistol-shot away even in the darkness. The ghostly curve of the main course above him was taut and motionless, filled with the steady breeze. Wind and weather were as favourable as he could wish for this passage, which he would not have attempted by night in thick or stormy conditions. It was reasonably certain that *Cracker* could have passed the narrows unscathed in daylight, but it was preferable that a British gun-brig should enter the Baltic unobserved if possible; the Danes must know by now that gun-brigs were being used as convoy escorts, and the sight of an inward-bound brig might alert them for an attempt on the outward convoy they could expect a few days later.

The chart pinned on the table in his cabin was clear in Mr Fitton's mind, but he pictured now the larger map of the Baltic and its shores. Not for the first time, he wondered at the extraordinary freak of nature by which a great arm of the sea, 1,000 miles long, was almost sealed off from the outer oceans by a barrier of land 150 miles across, and accessible only by one of the three narrow channels that pierced the barrier. You steered north-east into the Skagerrak, doubled the Skaw and sailed south up the Kattegat, to be brought up short by this opposing barrier of eastern Denmark, cut into two huge islands by those dividing channels. The central channel, the Great Belt, you would not attempt unless you were a Baltic seaman in a shallow-draught galliot, for the gut between Funen and Zealand was a maze of ill-charted shoals. The Little Belt farther to the west boasted a continuous deep channel, but it was exceedingly narrow and winding and a very roundabout way of getting from the Kattegat into the Baltic. Moreover, in this present time of war both entrances ushered a British vessel into the heart of a hostile country—or rather (Mr Fitton amended his thought) a country whose king had sworn allegiance to Bonaparte under threat of invasion and was now "monitored" by a representative of the Emperor.

The remaining channel, the Sound for which *Cracker* was heading, was by far the shortest route to the Baltic coast of Sweden and the handiest for a sailing-ship; you had practically a straight north-south run, which meant that with the prevailing westerlies you could enter or leave the Baltic with a fair wind. And here there was only one enemy shore to the channel. Sweden, surprisingly and resolutely neutral under an adopted ruler who had been one of the Emperor's marshals, offered no aid or refuge on the opposite, eastern, shore but would not interfere with the passage of a British ship.

"Good morning, sir."

Mr Fitton turned with a start to the dark shape that had materialised out of the darkness at his side. He could almost feel the wind of Mr Honeyburn's salute.

"Eight bells," continued the lieutenant, raising his reedy voice above the ceaseless plainsong of the wind, "the hour of your relief as officer of the watch, sir. I take over the deck."

"I'd no idea the morning was so far advanced," Mr Fitton said repentantly. "I had intended to send a hand below to tell you not to stir, since I shall remain on deck until we're past Kronenburg."

"But I would have stirred, you know," said Honeyburn with a chuckle. "I'm always glad to take the morning watch. Why, its very name is a poem. 'The beauty of the morning—silent, bare—' "

"Just so, Mr Honeyburn. We'll keep the watch together, then. I'll have a lookout at the foremasthead to report when he sees any light ahead. It'll probably be on the port bow. Will you see to that, if you please?"

Honeyburn delivered his windmill salute and departed. Mr Fitton, wondering why he always felt it necessary to speak gently to his second-in-command, walked across to the helm.

"Your trick's over, Mr Sholto, but I want you at the wheel until we sight Helsingborg. I'll have you relieved then."

"Aye aye, sir. I'm game for a double trick if you want."

"No need. Another hour should do it."

Mr Fitton returned to the weather rail and began to pace up and down in the darkness, aware after a minute or two that Mr Honeyburn was doing the same a few yards away on the port side. He would not have thought of objecting if the only other officer on board had chosen to join him; but the punctilious Honeyburn knew that the weather side of the quarterdeck was customarily the walking-place of the captain and had accordingly betaken himself to the lee side. For a moment he thought of asking the lieutenant to join him, though he had no wish for conversation. Then he dismissed the idea. Honeyburn would neither expect the invitation nor be in the least pained by the lack of it. So the two paced their ten steps for'ard and ten steps aft in the darkness as if they were acolytes performing some ritual of the night, with Sholto at the wheel amidships acting hierophant.

A little before two bells a hail from the masthead reported a light fine on the port bow. Twenty minutes later the few scattered lights of Helsingborg were visible from the deck and Mr Fitton, having replaced Sholto with a new quartermaster, bore slightly away to head straight for the Swedish port. The pallor of the false dawn was glimmering above the coast when he estimated his distance from the lights as one mile and put his helm down. The scattered yellow sparks on shore slid round on the beam as the gun-brig settled on her course due south, and then drifted farther and farther astern as she sailed on through the pitchy darkness that preceded true daybreak. There were no lights to starboard, where Elsinore and the guns of the Kronenburg fortress gave no sign of their existence to eye or ear. Grey light came slowly over the clouded sky and revealed the low hills of the Swedish coast close on the port hand, Denmark a dark receding line on the horizon to starboard, and the Swedish island of Hven raising its green hump above bronze-coloured cliffs ahead. Beyond Hven full day had come and the brown sails of small sailing-craft moved on the grey-green waters of Lundakra Bay; but already the coasts on either hand were four or five miles distant and soon they were only visible to the masthead lookout. *Cracker* had virtually passed the Sound, and with less incident than a beat up the Thames would have afforded.

Honeyburn, sent below to get his breakfast when the hands tumbled-up for the forenoon watch, was on deck again in twenty minutes to insist with courteous firmness that his commander should take his turn. Mr Fitton made no objection. There was one last piece of easy pilotage ahead, where the channel narrowed between some shallows and the low flat island of Saltholm, but Honeyburn could at least be trusted to keep close in to Saltholm; it was Danish territory but un-inhabited, being nothing more than a grassgrown sandbank six miles off the Copenhagen shore. So Mr Fitton went below for the first time in eight hours, glad enough of his cabin chair and a platter of oatmeal porridge.

He should, he knew, have been pleased with his success. It meant that he could safely shepherd his convoy—eight ships, he had been told to expect—northward through the Sound by night, given a favourable wind. But somehow he could find no satisfaction in prospect or retrospect. The humdrum six days across the North Sea with the two ships for Gothenburg and the easy and entirely uneventful passage of the Sound were going to be succeeded by an equally trouble-free return, he foresaw. He was thinking of those bygone years in the blue Caribbean when every cruise was a life-or-death hazard, when he was hunting the enemy instead of sneaking past him by night, when he had made the names of his little fighting-ships —*Ferret* and *Active*, *Gipsy* and *Pitt*—bywords on the West Indies station and far beyond it; when the hairsbreadth between survival and oblivion had made life a thousand times

B

worth living, an infinitely better thing than this Baltic creeping—

Mr Fitton pulled himself up, with a rueful grin at his own folly. This was too much like an old man's idealisation of past adventures, which had in fact been unimportant, bloody, and highly uncomfortable. *Know what you are, and behave according to that knowledge,* said Epictetus. Well, he was an elderly lieutenant now, concerned solely with doing his duty; and that duty was to bring a convoy of merchant ships back to England with as little hazard as possible.

Mr Fitton finished his porridge and the mug of Mr Grattan's excellent coffee and got out the chart of the south Baltic. With this steady wind on her beam *Cracker* had little to fear from any Danish gunboats that might be lurking in the bight south of Copenhagen. Twenty miles beyond Saltholm he could hug the Swedish coast to get round the Falsterbo peninsula, the southernmost point of Sweden, and then there remained only the run due east to his rendezvous west of Bornholm island. If the wind didn't fail him he should be there on the morning of the 3rd, a day later than had been appointed but well within the three days' latitude allowed him. The eight ships would be at the rendezvous by now, and he hoped their eight captains would be amenable to the orders of a British naval lieutenant; merchant skippers of whatever nationality were the most cantankerous breed on the face of the earth and (not unnaturally) reluctant to submit the direction of their vessels to anyone but themselves. That, however, was the only problem he would have to tackle, if indeed it arose at all. The return voyage—

An explosion, dull but heavy, ended his reflections abruptly. Before he reached the cabin door a second and a third gun fired from somewhere ahead of the gun-brig. Honeyburn's high-pitched voice yelled orders, feet thudded on the deck overhead, and *Cracker* heeled sharply over to starboard. He ran

34

up the ladder and onto the quarterdeck. Erikson, the bearded seaman at the helm, shot an apprehensive glance at him but his own gaze went instantly to the shore a mile distant on the starboard quarter. Saltholm was a long line of greenish brown on the ruffled grey water; smoke-clouds drifted above a hump that showed among the marram-grass flats.

"I ventured to alter course, sir," said Honeyburn, with the inevitable salute; his long bony face wore an expression of mild surprise. "The Danes have mounted a battery on Saltholm since we were here last. 12-pounders. The shot fell short, but since we were within range—"

"Just so." Mr Fitton was curt and impassive. "You altered course away, in so doing heading her straight for shoal water. —Helm a-starboard, Erikson. Steady.—Mr Honeyburn, I'll thank you to set a leadsman to work at once."

The lieutenant, who had been standing aghast with a hand clapped to his mouth and his eyes bulging, turned and dashed away as the bos'n came hurrying aft.

"Pipe all hands, Mr Sholto. I'll have the starboard guns run out and gun-crews closed up."

"Aye aye, sir."

Sholto's red head bobbed down with curious rapidity. A 12-pounder ball had whistled across the quarterdeck a few feet from the mainmast, just clearing the rail and doing no damage. The bos'n trotted away, his abashed and crimson face averted as he passed a seaman carrying the leadline coiled in his hand. Mr Fitton was watching for the next salvos. They came almost together, raising two jets of white water a stone's-throw ahead of the gun-brig and so nearly on her future position that it was clear those Danish gunners knew their business.

In putting *Cracker* back on her course parallel to the shore-line of Saltholm he had brought the enemy battery precisely on her starboard beam, and though the three guns were firing at long range and *Cracker* was making a good seven knots with this freshening wind they could reach her with their next discharge. The deck vibrated under his feet as the six guns of the starboard broadside rumbled out on their trucks, and the shout of the leadsman chanting his first sounding rose above the noise.

"By the mark two!"

Twelve feet of water—and *Cracker* drew more than ten!

"Starboard a point, Erikson," he said quickly to the man at the wheel; the main channel must be regained even though it meant closing the range for the Danish battery.

Just as well he had given that earlier helm order when he did. With the gun-brig aground on a shoal the 12-pounders could have played ducks-and-drakes with her at their leisure.

"Deep four!"

All was well, then; the underwater bank must be steep-to here. Mr Fitton made this deduction without taking his gaze from the distant hump of the battery, now falling astern, and hard on his thought his eye caught the three orange flashes, nearly together and bright in the dull atmosphere. Simultaneously with the two white fountains that rose out of the furrows of the gun-brig's wake came the jarring crash of a hit. The ball had struck somewhere on her quarter below deck-level by the feel of it.

"Carpenter's party, come aft here!" he shouted; and when Mr Trapp and his two men came running, "Below decks, starboard side—try Mr Honeyburn's cabin."

A 12-pounder ball finding its target at extreme range had spent much of its striking force; depending on how close it was to the waterline, it might with luck be easily repairable.

"Deep four!" came the leadsman's shout again.

"Port helm," he told the helmsman. "Steady as you go."

Cracker, again on her proper course down the channel, must

36

surely be out of range now—and here came the fourth discharge to test it. Three splashes one after the other and all half-a-cable away on the quarter. If that battery fired again he could ignore it—but it might not be the only battery on Saltholm. Mr Fitton sent his powerful voice to the lookout high on the foremast.

"Masthead, there! Why didn't you report the battery when you saw it?'

A pause. "Saw a 'ump, sir—didn't know 'twas a battery."

That was young Weldon, pressed two months ago and fresh out of the receiving-ship; probably he'd never seen a battery before or heard an enemy gun fired.

"You'll know the next one, Weldon. Keep your eyes skinned."

But what had *Courageux* and the two frigates been about to allow the Danes to establish a battery here? *Cracker* was lucky to have got off as lightly as she had done. However, a hole in her quarter was a small price to pay for the knowledge that the Saltholm channel was commanded by enemy guns; knowledge sufficiently disturbing to a sea-officer who was proposing to take a large convoy out of the Baltic by way of that channel.

3

The gun-brig was making eight knots with the stronger beam wind that had sprung up north of Saltholm, and in five minutes it was clear that she was beyond all danger from batteries on land. The low dun-coloured shore of the flats was fast receding as the channel trended east of south. Mr Fitton ordered the leadsman out of the chains and the guns hauled in and secured. As Sholto piped down and the hands of the watch-below vanished down the fore hatchway Mr Honeyburn confronted his commander. His face, as long as a fiddle and not

37

unlike one, looked more puzzled than guilty but he was plainly conscious that he had earned a reprimand.

"Sir," he said resolutely, " 'my apprehensions crowd upon me.' Wordsworth. I deplore my error. But how I came to forget the shoals to port—well, I did forget the shoals to port and there you have it."

It was on the tip of Mr Fitton's tongue to say, "A sea-officer who can forget a shoal under his lee had better stay ashore," but he could not be properly angry with Honeyburn.

" 'To err is human,' Mr Honeyburn," he said, giving the lieutenant a Pope for his Wordsworth. "The graver fault is to make the same error twice. I'm sure you'll see to it that—well, Mr Trapp?"

He broke off his admonition, not without some relief, and turned to the carpenter, an elderly man with a wizened brown face and an impressive manner of speech.

"The henemy ball, sir," said Mr Trapp, "struck but a glarncing blow—a glarncing blow. It did not penetrate, seeing as how by a fortnit charnce—a fortnit charnce, sir, it struck where the planking crorses the third rib-timber from the starn. The planking there is stove-in over a harea of three foot by two—"

"Above waterline?" interrupted Mr Fitton.

Mr Trapp looked pained. " 'Ad it not been, sir, I would 'ave reported himmediately. 'Arf a fathom above waterline it is, and through it you may see the light o' day—the daylight, sir, from the hinterior of Mr Honeyburn's cabin."

Mr Honeyburn was heard to murmur that it was extremely naughty of the Danes.

"Timmis and Johns is rectifying the defect now," pursued the carpenter. "Rectifying the defect, that's to say, temporairily, sir. For the work outboard I'll 'ave to wait till she's at anchor."

"Very good, Mr Trapp. Carry on." Mr Fitton turned to his

lieutenant. "Secure guns, Mr Honeyburn, and send down all hands except the watch, if you please. I have the remainder of the forenoon watch, so I advise you to get some sleep. In my cabin," he added as the hammering of Mr Trapp and his mates sounded from below.

"Thank you." Honeyburn hesitated. "I—um—was expecting your order to open fire on that battery, sir."

"I'll thank you to have those guns secured, Mr Honeyburn," Mr Fitton said severely, with a frown that sent the lieutenant hastily about his business.

His second-in-command neither deserved an explanation nor should he have needed one. The 18-pounder carronades, with an effective range of half-a-mile, could have done nothing whatever against the Danish battery, and the starboard 4-pounder long gun (the mounting of which in *Cracker* had cost her commander a long struggle with the dockyard) would have been equally ineffective against those solid breastworks and parapets. Having the guns run out had been partly a showing of teeth and partly a measure to preserve the morale of his crew; seamen were only happy under fire when their own means of retaliation were, at the least, displayed and ready.

The gun-brig sped on across green waters under a grey sky, eating up her southing towards the point where she would turn east for the Bornholm rendezvous. Honeyburn had gone below and except for Garroway at the wheel Mr Fitton had the quarterdeck to himself. The southern end of Saltholm was in sight, a mere line just clearing the horizon on the starboard bow, and with his glass he could make out the string of little islets called the Svan-klapperne that ran out from it towards the fairway. He judged the distance, took a bearing with the hand-compass, and told Garroway to give her half-a-point more of easting. *Cracker* was about to enter the southern corner of the Baltic and unless he was imagining it the air was noticeably colder. These waters merged with those of the Gulf of Finland and the Gulf of Bothnia, the latter reaching nearly as far north as the Arctic Circle and receiving the icy rivers of Lapland, so the sea itself was colder than the North Sea and not so salty. It was early October now; in three months' time the two Gulfs would be frozen over and ice could be a danger as far south as Stockholm. Once in the last century, he had heard, the Sound itself had frozen and folk had walked across from Denmark to Sweden. No wonder he felt cold. He was on the point of calling one of the hands from for'ard to fetch up his pea-jacket when he remembered that Honeyburn was sleeping in his cabin—if he was able to sleep with the carpenters hammering a few feet away. Instead, he began to pace briskly up and down, considering the while the matter of the Saltholm battery.

It had taken a considerable time for that battery to be established where it was. On a bank of sand like Saltholm there would have to be solid emplacements and workmen would have to construct these with materials brought by sea from Copenhagen. Then there were the 12-pounders themselves, the ammunition for them and its storage, the gunners and some sort of quarters for them—all coming round by sea, most probably in barges. How had all this activity over a longish period escaped the notice of Admiral Saumarez's squadron?

Either *Clio* or *Hamadryad* would be patrolling the southern approaches to the Sound at least once in a week, on the lookout for just such signs that the Danes were stirring into action. A frigate's 18-pounders could have silenced the Danish battery with ease, or failing that a broadside or two from *Courageux* could have pounded it into dust. Sir James Saumarez, Mr Fitton knew, was ill and had gone home to England; it looked as though Captain Anderson, commanding in his absence, was failing in his duty. And what of his convoy? All eight ships were bound to be larger and of deeper draught

40

than his little gun-brig and the danger of their running aground was consequently greater. By day they would have to run the gauntlet of the 12-pounder battery one by one, and even at night a procession of nine vessels could scarcely hope to pass undetected. Moreover, he would have to sound his way past Saltholm if he decided to try the passage in darkness, and for that he would need very favourable conditions of wind and sea if he or one of his charges were not to run aground. No; the battery must be put out of action, either by gunfire or by a landing-party of marines from *Courageux*, before he took his convoy past Saltholm. Mr Fitton was considering how to frame an urgent request to Captain Anderson when the lookout hailed from the masthead.

"Deck, there! Small craft ahead, south o' the islands—pulling-boats, sir, five or six on 'em."

Mr Fitton saw that the outermost islet of the Svan-klapperne was now less than a mile distant, fine on the starboard bow, and the implications of what he had heard sent him dashing along the deck and up the weather shrouds of the foremast with an agility that denied his self-portrait as an elderly lieutenant. Weldon had swarmed up to sit on the fore top-gallant yard with his arms locked round the mast. His commander locked knee and elbow into the ratlines just below him and steadied his glass, looking past the curved edge of the sail, on the brown sandbank at the outer end of the chain.

"I see no boats," he called to Weldon.

"They went be'ind the bank yonder, sir. You'd say they was—see there, sir! Another on 'em."

Mr Fitton had seen. The islet, its crest perhaps twenty feet above the sea, was fifty or sixty feet long and separated from the next in the chain by a gap of similar length; a boat had pulled rapidly across this intervening water to vanish behind the sandbank—a large boat heavily manned and mounting a gun in its bows. It did not reappear.

41

"You've sharp eyes, Weldon," said Mr Fitton, pocketing his glass. "Down to the deck with you—I'll need all hands."

He swung down the ratlines at a speed that left Weldon far above and began issuing his orders as soon as his feet touched the deck.

"Pass the word for Mr Sholto. Higgs, go to my cabin and rouse Mr Honeyburn—my compliments and I'll be glad if he'll come on deck." And to the bos'n as he came running up, "Pipe all hands, Mr Sholto—action stations, all guns cleared away, all guns load."

"Aye aye, sir. Ball, sir?"

"Number Six guns port and starboard load grape, the rest ball."

The bos'n's silver "call" squealed ear-piercingly. Mr Fitton ran aft to the helm.

"Bring her closer to the wind, Garroway—steady."

Cracker would pass within three cable lengths of the islet on a course at right-angles to its length. At the rate she was sailing there was little time to spare; it was on occasions like this that he felt the need for more executive officers. But here came Honeyburn, with his jacket half pulled-on and his breeches imperfectly buttoned. And the deck was vibrating to the trampling of feet and the thunder of the gun-trucks.

"Gunboats, Mr Honeyburn. Half-a-dozen or so in ambush behind the bank there."

"Good gracious!" said Honeyburn, blinking and tugging at his sleeves.

"Just so. Take charge of the guns, if you please. Those of the starboard broadside will fire as each gun bears. I needn't tell you that accurate aim is of the first importance now."

"Trust me, sir," responded Honeyburn happily; he saluted less wildly than usual and galloped away along the deck.

Gunnery was one of the very few things in which Honeyburn could be trusted as a sea-officer. In the present emergency that was just as well. In attacking a larger vessel gunboats made up for their small size and one-gun armament by their ability to bring their guns instantly to bear on the target without depending on the wind. They could not, of course, give chase to a fast brig like *Cracker*; their first shots would be aimed to bring down a spar or disable the helm. Then, with their prey broached-to or losing way, they could either manoeuvre so as to pound her stern or quarters, or dash alongside to board. A boarding-party from four gunboats would outnumber *Cracker*'s men by two to one. Mr Fitton, therefore, proposed to hit the enemy as hard as he could before showing his heels.

He glanced for'ard along the deck where the gun-crews stood ready and the smoke from the smouldering slow-matches drifted thinly above the planking. Undermanned as she was, the gun-brig could only provide full crews for one broadside, the other six guns remaining ready and in charge of a gunlayer until they were needed. Honeyburn was dodging along the fully-manned starboard guns, stooping and pointing and admonishing with visible enthusiasm. Mr Fitton turned his attention to the islet, less than half-a-mile away and swiftly drawing abeam. No doubt hoping to achieve a complete surprise, the Danes had mustered their boats close in behind the long bank of sand so that they were still hidden from sight. So much the better—it meant that the gunboats would be bunched together. Honeyburn had stopped bobbing up and down like a jack-in-a-box and was crouching motionless by Number One gun, the 4-pounder nearest the bows. The tip of the islet came abeam and suddenly the enemy swung into sight on its farther side, five gunboats in a close pack, oars flailing as the rowers gave way. Precisely as his eye fell on them *Cracker*'s 4-pounder and one of the Danish guns exploded simultaneously and the fight was on.

It was all over in sixty seconds. The first enemy shot plumped into the sea under the gun-brig's bows and Mr Fitton saw the splash of the 4-pounder ball well astern of the advancing boats. He had scarcely time to damn Honeyburn for allowing insufficient depression when the carronades began to fire one by one. A Danish ball hummed across the deck amidships and another opened a neat hole in the bottom of the mainsail, but Honeyburn was doing better than that with his carronades. One shot smashed the oars on the port side of the leading gunboat and it instantly slewed round in confusion, fouling a second boat that was too close on its quarter and involving the boat astern in a triple collision. Another 18-pounder ball—from Number Four gun, he thought—passed across a fourth boat, too high to strike the hull but low enough to hurl three of the oarsmen overboard in a tangle of bloody rags and splintered oars.

"Stand aside, man!" screeched Honeyburn with unwonted vigour.

He thrust past the gunlayer of Number Six gun, the after carronade that was loaded with grape, and fiddled with the screw of the quoin. The fifth and last gunboat had drawn far ahead of its disabled companions and was foaming through the water towards the brig, hardly more than two hundred yards away. Mr Fitton could see the gunners working frantically to reload the bow gun. Honeyburn stood back quickly from the carronade.

"Fire!"

The belch of flame and smoke seemed to wither the oncoming craft as if by magic. The toiling figures vanished or crumpled, the boat swerved and lay listing heavily, a chorus of screams and cries came down the wind. Mr Fitton turned an impassive face to the helmsman.

"Bear away now. Steer south a point east."

"South a point east it is, sir."

Cracker sped on under a grey noonday sky with the steady wind abaft the beam and Saltholm already a hazy grey streak astern. The Danish gunboats, or what was left of them, dwindled and passed from sight. Mr Fitton made his powerful voice carry far for'ard.

"Well done, my lads. We've given the Danes a double ration of shot and it's dead on eight bells of the forenoon watch. Mr Sholto, double rum ration to every man—see to it." He gave time for the inevitable cheering, then topped it with a brisker shout. "All guns secure!"

A scarecrow figure with wrinkled stockings and hat comically awry saluted him. It was very evident that Honeyburn's struggles with certain buttons had been unsuccessful.

"Pray accept my felicitations on your excellent shooting, Mr Honeyburn," he said formally. "I've rarely seen better."

The lieutenant, equally embarrassed by reprimand or commendation, sought refuge in his favourite poet.

" 'Sometimes with thoughts of very bliss I catch at them, and then I miss,' " he said modestly.

"But I must ask, with your leave"—Mr Fitton paused to steady his voice—"that you do something about your breeches. Or else, sir, we shall all be shamed."

He turned away, hiding a grin, while Honeyburn hastily betook himself to the lee rail to adjust his dress. But the grin quickly faded. All very well to have cleared the Sound and have a dozen miles of safe water on either hand. All very well to make the return passage, chancing gunboats and batteries, if he had only his own little command to think of. But it was much more than likely that there were plenty of other gunboats to replace those he had disabled—and how could one gun-brig defend eight merchant ships against a determined attack by gunboats? It was a question he would ask Captain Anderson of the *Courageux*.

THREE

The Convoy

I

George Clewes, master of the merchant ship *Dragon*, lounged on the padded stern thwart of his smart longboat in the best of tempers.

"Put your bloody backs into it, you bastards," he said genially, addressing the six deckhands who were straining at the oars. "The God-damned British Navy's watching you."

Since five of them were Scandinavians and the sixth a Pole, he added an oath or two in Swedish. Mr Clewes, though born in Essex, considered himself a citizen of the world.

The longboat was pulling towards the gun-brig that had just let go her anchor. It was barely two hours after sunrise in October, but the warmth of the sun made itself felt through the steamy haze that lay across the waters of the Baltic. Those waters were palest blue and rippled by the light breeze, which was beginning to disperse the vapours and open gaps in them through which could be seen a sky totally devoid of cloud. The grey overcast of the past two days had cleared during the night, making way for one of those perfect Baltic mornings which in early autumn seem to scoff at the idea of an approaching winter. Captain Clewes (he exacted the courtesy rank on all occasions) threw aside his furred top-coat and turned to glance astern. A gap had opened in the wavering white mists and the eight anchored vessels shone clear in the sunlight, their brown hulls low in the blue water under the burden of a full lading. All were three-masters, ship-rigged. To Captain Clewes's eye, his own *Dragon* stood out from the seven Swedish ships like a thoroughbred among cart-horses with her white cordage, glistening new paintwork, and the twinkle of sunlight on the two cannon on her fo'csle. He blew out his heavy jowls in a sigh of self-approbation and swung round to cast a disparaging eye on the little brig, now close ahead.

Captain Clewes had about him something of the flash and glitter of his ship, and would have been delighted to be told so. He was a large man, red-cheeked and black-whiskered, and the fingers that rested on his thighs (clad in the tightest of white breeches) sparkled with rings of undoubted value. His blue coat and the cocked hat which he wore dashingly tilted over one ear suggested that he considered himself the equal of any naval post-captain, and suggested correctly; Captain Clewes, indeed, felt himself capable of filling an admiral's post, and often regretted that the merchant service had no admirals. His present good-humour, however, had no under-tone of regret. The cargo he had brought out from England to Riga had won him a profit of two hundred per cent—for he was owner as well as master—and to the almost equally profitable venture of taking wheat from Riga to Stockholm had been added a fortunate chance of returning to England with a full load of timber and a naval escort.

"Lay me alongside smartly, damn you!" said Captain Clewes amiably. "Or by God I'll have some of you in irons."

The longboat sheered under *Cracker*'s port quarter as the starboard oarsmen boated oars. Captain Clewes heaved himself up the short ladder with a reckless display of agility and sprang down, puffing somewhat, to the gun-brig's quarterdeck. He found himself confronting a stocky broad-shouldered man

47

who wore the single epaulette of a naval lieutenant on the shoulder of his salt-stained blue coat. The lieutenant's brown face, as squarecut as the rest of him, was deeply lined at the corners of eyes and mouth and furrowed by an old scar that ran from ear to jaw on the left cheek. The two men saluted.

"Fitton, lieutenant in command," said the gun-brig's officer. "Welcome aboard, sir."

"Clewes of the *Dragon*," said his visitor graciously, "Captain George Clewes. I'm directed by Lord Romsey to deliver these dispatches to you instantly upon your arrival, lieutenant." He handed over a thin oblong wrapped in oilskin. "You were expected yesterday."

"I was delayed," said Mr Fitton briefly, taking the packet.

Lord Romsey was the British Ambassador to the Royal Court at Stockholm, an unlikely personage to issue orders regarding a gun-brig's convoy duties. Where, then, was *Courageux*? The morning mists had lifted, the ruffled blue stretched clear to the horizon, and the eight merchantmen at anchor were the only vessels in sight.

Clewes was staring round him with a critical air, noting the spotless deck, the hands for'ard rigging the clothes-lines for their laundry, the three men squatting amidships patching a hole in the sail whose folds lay across their legs. From overside on the starboard quarter, where Mr Trapp and one of his men dangled on a bos'n's chair, came the sound of hammering.

"Glad to see you keep 'em at it, lieutenant," he said. "Hard work and the cat—that's the ticket."

Mr Fitton made no answer to this. "May I ask if you've seen anything of the British squadron, sir?" he demanded.

"Not a sign," Clewes answered. "I fancy you'll find an explanation in that packet," he added.

"Pray come down to my cabin, Mr Clewes. You'll take a glass of wine?"

Clewes followed him down the ladder and ducked into the

little cabin, his thick lips curling as his eye took in its bareness and lack of comforts. His host got a bottle and glasses from the locker and having excused himself left the captain to sample the Madeira while he opened the oilskin packet. The letter inside was sealed with the royal arms. He broke the seal and read its contents.

STOCKHOLM

HIS BRITANNIC MAJESTY'S EMBASSY

25th September 1812

Sir,

In view of the news, just received, of Bonaparte's entry into Moscow, and the possibility of a further Russian retreat towards the west, the three vessels of the British Baltic Squadron have been ordered to the Gulf of Finland, to afford assistance to the Russians should this be practicable. Your instructions therefore emanate from this Embassy instead of from the officer commanding the Squadron. You are directed to sail as convoy escort as previously arranged. The vessels to be escorted are as follows: *Dalarna*, *Ingria*, *Blanzeflor*, *Frithiof*, *Iduna*, *Ahund Jakob*, *Anjala*, Swedish merchantmen; *Dragon*, British merchantman. You will lose no time in proceeding off the Nore with your convoy. All eight vessels carry timber which is understood to be in urgent demand in the naval dockyards.

ROMSEY

His Britannic Majesty's

Ambassador in Stockholm

Mr Fitton read the dispatch a second time and lingered, frowning slightly, on the final sentence; this was the first indication he had been given that this convoy was of special importance. Of greater moment, however, was the news that the South Baltic had been empty of British warships for more than a week. It was not to be doubted that Copenhagen would have spies in Stockholm, and the Danes would hasten to push forward their defences—especially in the neighbourhood of the

Sound—the instant they knew their coasts were free from British surveillance. It could well be that *Cracker*'s fortuitous encounter with the battery and the gunboats had been a brush with the outposts of much larger forces that were preparing for aggressive action when the next westbound convoy should approach the Sound. In any case, now that the assistance he had hoped for from *Courageux* was barred to him the plan of taking a convoy out through the Sound must be ruled out of consideration.

"Boney's in Moscow—that's your news, hey?" said Clewes; his glass was empty and he pushed it across the table. "It's bad. Sweden won't come in against France if Russia's defeated—I had that from Romsey's own lips."

Mr Fitton refilled the glass, not without slight misgiving; the captain's breath when he came on board had testified of brandy. "The Ambassador has explained the absence of *Courageux* and the frigates," he said, "and I'm instructed that the convoy is to sail as soon as may be. There'll have to be a conference of ships' captains but it shouldn't take long. Can you be on board here at noon?"

"I can but I won't." Clewes gulped half his wine. "You can't seat nine men in this hutch, man. Hold your conference on board *Dragon*—you could give a ball in my stern cabin, and there'll be no bloody banging going on."

"My carpenter will be finished by noon," said Mr Fitton.

"What's more, I've plenty of schnapps," Clewes went on unheeding. "This stuff's very fair, but these Stockholm skippers like stronger liquor. You speak Swedish?"

"Half-a-dozen words. Not enough for this purpose."

"You're lucky. I can *tala* like any bloody Swede—there's nine of 'em in my crew, not to mention three Danes and a couple of French. Noon on board *Dragon*, then—that's clinched." The captain flourished his glass, which was once more empty. "We'll drink to it."

50

Disguising his reluctance, Mr Fitton poured more of his Madeira. Much as he disliked Clewes's manner of suggesting it a conference in some less confined space than this cabin was obviously preferable. Usually all that had to be done at such meetings was to ensure that every captain understood the code of signals to be used in manoeuvring and the necessity of conforming to the escort's directions; but at the coming conference he would have to explain why he would not be taking the convoy through the Sound. Clewes's familiarity with the Swedish language would come in useful there if the captain was as fluent as he claimed to be. He saw no reason why Clewes should have it explained to him before the conference; he would learn about it then, in his capacity as interpreter.

Clewes, with his tongue now well loosened, was holding forth with a good deal of bombast about the international situation in the Baltic, retailing the gossip he had picked up on the Stockholm quays and (so he said) from the British Ambassador. Mr Fitton stole a glance at his watch and decided to allow him ten minutes more and then get rid of him so that he could prepare for the conference.

Bernadotte (said Clewes) was more than half ready to declare war on Bonaparte. The Crown Prince, as he was styled in Sweden, had been furious when the Emperor took his army through Swedish Pomerania and was only awaiting the result of the conflict with Russia; a Russian defeat would place Sweden in such danger that she would have to remain neutral, but if Napoleon was forced back from Moscow she would certainly move to attack the French. As for the Danes, their king was too tightly under Bonaparte's thumb to change sides now.

"The buzz is", Clewes went on, "that this Baron La Haye don't move a yard from King Christian's elbow. You've heard of La Haye, of course."

51

Mr Fitton admitted that the name was unfamiliar, and ignored the empty glass that was being waggled insinuatingly under his nose. Clewes shook his head pityingly.

"You must recall La Haye, lieutenant—you're old enough. *Emigré* aristocrat twenty years ago, lived in England till Boney decided to be a bloody emperor, then cut his stick and hopped back to France. Got himself into Boney's good books and now he's one of his right-hand men and lord high arse-creeper to the King of Denmark. They say Christian would have second thoughts about his alliance with the French if La Haye wasn't there to keep him up to scratch."

Mr Fitton nodded. He was more concerned with his own immediate problems than with King Christian's, and had only half an ear to spare for the merchant captain's further retailing of Stockholm rumour. The Danish court, it appeared, had moved from Copenhagen in August and was still at the King's mansion near the port of Svendborg—"King, Baron, Baron's daughter, and all," said Clewes. The daughter had married Marshal Brennier, who had been killed at Ciudad Rodrigo, as Fitton must surely remember. They'd all left the capital, according to the Ambassador, on account of the riots in protest against Danish regiments being sent to Russia. Broken windows at the palace—

At this point Captain Clewes perceived, despite the effects of Madeira on top of much brandy, that he had none of Mr Fitton's attention.

"Well, you're not interested," he said, picking up his hat, "and you're damned right, lieutenant. What's it to you and me, so long as the bloody war goes on?"

"Goes on?" repeated Mr Fitton, his notice attracted by the question.

"Surely—goes on." Clewes crouched ostentatiously as he went out through the doorway. "When it stops you'll be on half-pay, I take it—and I'll lose the best trade I ever had.

D'you know what cargo I took out to Riga? Forty thousand pairs of Northampton boots and shoes."

"For the Russian army, I suppose," Mr Fitton observed as they came up onto the sunlit quarterdeck.

The captain chuckled. "It's not my business where they went, but I'll lay a hundred to one they went to Moscow—and not on Russian feet, either." He paused with a hand on the rail. "Noon on board my ship. Until then, *farval*, as they say in these parts."

He clambered down into his boat and was presently heard cursing the oarsmen as they pulled away from *Cracker*'s side.

" 'A creature not too bright or good' ", murmured a voice.

Mr Fitton turned, repressing a grin. "Criticism of merchant captains ill becomes us, Mr Honeyburn. Even if it's William Wordsworth's voice. Have you anything to report?"

"Minor details, sir," said Honeyburn. "Repairs to mains'l complete. Wind's veering northerly, and glass is steady."

In these waters a northerly veer with a steady glass usually meant clear and cold weather with a wind from the east. It was all that was needed to confirm the difficult decision he had already taken.

"Have the jolly-boat hove-out and manned fifteen minutes before noon, if you please," said Mr Fitton. "I shall be going on board *Dragon* for the convoy conference."

"Aye aye, sir."

"And Mr Honeyburn—see that all's ready for getting under way. The convoy will sail at four bells of the afternoon watch."

2

At two bells of the afternoon watch Mr Fitton was experiencing some doubt concerning the confident statement of sailing time he had made to his second-in-command. The atmosphere in Clewes's spacious stern cabin on board *Dragon*, blue with the smoke of strong tobacco and reeking of schnapps, did not add to his comfort as he glanced quickly round the table preparatory to putting forward his plan for the convoy route.

The cabin with its curtained ports and cushioned benches matched its owner but not the Swedish skippers who sat at the table with him. Two of them were youngish men and sported broadcloth jackets and cleanshaven chins, but the other five were middle-aged or elderly and clad in old fur-collared pea-jackets or the duffel tunics beloved of Swedish seamen. Reuterholm of the *Ahund Jakob* was the senior shipmaster present, an old man smaller than the others but evidently commanding their respect; his white beard was stained yellow with tobacco and from beneath the jutting eaves of his eyebrows a pair of very blue eyes stared disconcertingly at the British naval officer opposite him. Of the seven Swedes only one—Birger of the *Frithiof*—spoke any English. Mr Fitton had been reluctantly counting on Erikson, Norwegian by birth and able to get his tongue round Swedish, to interpret for him, and it was a relief to find that Clewes's boast of fluency in Swedish appeared to be no empty one. Through Clewes, he had first gone over the routine arrangement of signals, emphasising that the safety of each vessel in the convoy depended on her speedy conformity with orders signalled by the escort. He had anticipated some objection here but the assembled captains seemed to accept it without question. Next he had described *Cracker*'s passage of the Sound. This took some time, because the account of the battery on Saltholm and the attack by gunboats brought startled questions from Clewes and these had to be answered before he would pass on the story to the Swedes. Their dismay was evident, and doubly so when Mr Fitton's further information, that *Courageux* and the frigates were 600 miles away and unable to clear the enemy from the approaches of the Sound, was translated to them. While they debated the matter Captain Clewes (who had not been moderate with his own schnapps) had his own say in conference with the escort commander.

"It's a damned tricky puzzle, Fitton," he said hoarsely. "I know that channel. If you're thinking you can make the passage by night, with eight of us in your wake like a lot of bloody ducks, you're mad."

"I wasn't thinking of it."

"And by God it's just as well—you'd not have me with you! I'd take my cargo elsewhere."

"To Bonaparte, perhaps," suggested Mr Fitton impassively; he disliked being browbeaten.

Clewes, who was sitting next to him, gave him a sharp sidelong glance and then chuckled. "Well, and why not? It's fools that make wars and wise men that make money out of 'em. If I was to tell you the sweet little fortune I've got salted away, and how I came by it—" He checked himself quickly. "But you're a King's officer and think differently."

"Just so, Mr Clewes. I have my orders to obey, and those orders require me to take a convoy to England. We're wasting time. I'll thank you to ask our Swedish friends whether any one of them has experience of taking a vessel through the Little Belt."

"The Little—" Clewes choked and goggled at him. "By God, man, you'd be mad indeed to try that! Why, the channel winds like a bloody snake and the distance is three times as long as—"

"Have you sailed through the Little Belt, Mr Clewes?"

"No, but—"

"Then please to ask my question," said Mr Fitton incisively.

Captain Clewes blew out his red cheeks, scratched his head, and did as he was told. Mention of the Little Belt obviously disconcerted the Swedes and three of them began to argue.

Mr Fitton, waiting, caught Captain Reuterholm's piercing gaze fixed upon him with unnerving steadiness. The babble of Swedish ceased and Clewes turned to him.

"Nilsson made a passage through the Little Belt when he was a boy. Birger took his ship through four years ago, before the war, but he had a Danish pilot on board."

"*Ja, ja,*" put in Captain Birger, who was trying to follow the English words. "Pi-lot, must have. *Lille Boelt* is not good way."

"Birger's in the right of it," Clewes said pontifically. "You can rule that plan out of court, Fitton."

"Not just yet, Mr Clewes. You'll put my case to the Swedes first, if you please."

"But God damn it, man!" Clewes exploded. "Have you looked at the bloody map? Halfway through that passage you're in the middle of Denmark—a hundred miles of enemy country on your port hand, a hundred and fifty to starboard, and the ships within musket-shot of the shores most of the way. What's more—"

"I'm aware of all this, thank you. Perhaps you wish to advocate the Great Belt as an alternative?"

"What—with *Dragon*? God, no! Any fool knows the shoals are impassable with vessels of—"

"Then be silent, sir," said Mr Fitton sternly. "We waste time. Pray translate precisely as I speak."

Clewes opened his mouth, shut it again, and shrugged his shoulders. Mr Fitton began to talk and the captain interpreted sentence by sentence.

It was certain (said Mr Fitton) that any convoy attempting the Sound would suffer heavy losses. It was probable that every ship would be taken or destroyed. Since plans for the convoy had been talked of in Stockholm for a month or more the Danes would know of it by now. With no British warships to prevent them, they could prepare to intercept it in the Sound and had very likely made such preparations. Therefore

56

an alternative way must be sought. The shoals of the Great Belt forbade vessels as large as the Swedish ships to use it. There remained the Little Belt. (Here Mr Fitton picked up the rolled chart from beside his chair and spread it on the table.) This route, though long and winding, had a continuous fairway, a channel whose depth was never less than six fathoms. It had two sections where pilotage would be difficult —here where the islets of Aaro and Baago forced the channel into a narrow curve, north-east and north-west; and here, ten miles farther north, at the double bend before the outlet into wider waters and plain sailing. The Little Belt, it was true, led through the heart of hostile country. But it would be entirely unexpected that a convoy bound for England should use it, and the only real danger was at the extreme northern end where the fortress of Fredericia commanded the narrows.

"You'll please to add," Mr Fitton ended, "that I've held a Royal Navy certificate as master's mate for the past twenty years and I'm fully confident that with this—" he tapped the chart—"I can pilot the convoy through the Little Belt."

He sat back, waiting while this was translated. There was a brief silence when Clewes had finished. Then someone said "*Nej—nej*," and at once a clash of argument in Swedish broke out. Mr Fitton's face was impassive as usual, but inwardly he was extremely anxious. He might exact obedience to his signals when he was escorting the convoy under sail, but he could not order any of these captains—not even Clewes—to follow him through the Little Belt. If they all resolved to go back to Stockholm he could not stop them. He remembered the wording of the dispatch from the British Embassy: *All eight vessels carry timber which is understood to be in urgent demand in the naval dockyards.* Lieutenant Michael Fitton would have exerted himself to the utmost to bring a Baltic convoy safe to England even if it was a single vessel returning in ballast. With that hint of urgency to spur him he knew that success must be achieved, even though he had to exceed his duty to achieve it.

"*Stopp!*"

The voice of Captain Reuterholm, loudly raised, broke through the din of argument. The talk of the others died away and they faced him while he spoke two curt sentences which brought nods of approval from his fellow skippers. The old man turned to Clewes and spoke briefly, keeping his eyes on the naval lieutenant while he did so. Clewes translated.

"He says he don't believe you can take 'em through without a pilot who knows the channel—a Danish pilot, that'd be. He says they won't sail with you unless you take a pilot on board. And that's out of the question, so you may as well—"

"Ask him this," Mr Fitton broke in quickly. "If I produce that pilot before we enter the channel—off the Vejsnaes Nakke, let us say—will he and the others follow me through the Little Belt?"

It was a chance he had to take; the only chance. He found himself holding his breath as he watched the faces of the Swedish shipmasters. The weatherbeaten features, bearded or shaven, turned this way and that in grave debate. On some he thought he saw assent, on others doubt or indecision; but again it was old Reuterholm who summed-up for all.

"*Ja!*" said he, forcibly, and followed that with a dozen words sternly pronounced and emphasised by the stab of a horny forefinger.

"The old boy says they'll all sail on that condition," Clewes said uneasily. "He says he trusts the word of an Englishman. God help you if you can't keep it!"

"Those weren't Captain Reuterholm's words, I fancy."

"No. They're mine. I think you're a fool, Fitton."

Mr Fitton, who was slowly rolling up his chart, nodded absently. His thoughts were concentrated on working out a mathematical problem involving several factors, some of which were uncertain: distance, course, weather, wind force, probable speed of slowest ship, all the interacting circumstances that would give him the arrival time he was aiming at. He had planned to sail at the earliest opportunity, but he would have to put back his sailing time now. He became aware that the captain of the *Blanzeflor* was speaking.

"Ebbeson wants to know what time the convoy sails," said Clewes.

"Very well." His rough calculation would have to stand. "Please translate exactly, Mr Clewes. The signal to up-anchor and make sail will be two lights at *Cracker*'s masthead. The convoy will sail one hour after sunset."

As he had expected, there was some surprised murmuring at this; it meant a delay of five or six hours before sailing. He went on, quickly and firmly.

"The wind is fair for the Fehmarn Belt. We shall pass that and rendezvous in the Marstal Bugt, anchoring one mile south-east of the Vejnaes Nakke."

"We come in dark to Marstal Bugt," frowned Captain Birger, who had evidently been making his own calculations.

"The moon is half full, captain, and you all have charts and lead-lines. There should be no difficulty." He stood up, summoning two words from his very limited store of Swedish. "*Lycklig rasa!*"

The Swedes grinned, possibly at his faulty pronunciation, and some of them returned his wish for a lucky voyage; after which ensued a period of general hand-shaking and schnapps-drinking from which Mr Fitton contrived to escape early without undue discourtesy. It was necessary to thank Clewes for his hospitality and assistance, and that involved fending-off a number of questions which he was not yet prepared to answer. But at last he was over *Dragon*'s side and the jolly-boat was taking him back across the intervening blue water to the privacy of his own cabin, where he could do some concen-

59

trated thinking. In overcoming one problem he had provided himself with another. He had to find a pilot.

3

"La-a-and ho!" The lookout's hail drifted down from the masthead. "Port beam, sir!"

Mr Honeyburn, who had the morning watch, screeched an acknowledgement from the quarterdeck and sent a hand to rouse the gun-brig's commander. Mr Fitton, however, was on deck before the seaman had reached the hatchway. The sun was not yet up and *Cracker* was racing over a dark sea flecked with white crests, flying from the golden radiance that grew above the sea horizon far astern. Silhouetted against the clear sky of coming sunrise were four of the Swedish ships, under all plain sail and at varying distances from the brig; three others sailed in line abreast half-a-mile away on her quarter.

"Where's *Dragon*?" inquired Mr Fitton when he had responded to the lieutenant's sweeping salute.

"She was in sight ahead at first light, sir, with stuns'ls set." Mr Honeyburn coughed. " 'Spread like a fan to catch the breezy air', in the words of—"

"Out of sight now?"

"Yes, sir. Captain Clewes seems to think this is a race."

"Captain Clewes will shortly find he's mistaken," said Mr Fitton, frowning. "This land abeam will be the Arkona cape. We're on course and making better speed than I expected."

"The wind freshened a trifle at two bells, sir. It's still steady, just north of east."

"So I see." Mr Fitton stepped to the binnacle. "Yes. Keep her as she goes, Mr Honeyburn—course west-sou'-west and by west."

He went down again to his cabin and bent over the chart,

which was held flat on the table by his sheathed sword and a battered volume of Tampion's *Treatise on the Sextant*. As he did so the sun topped the horizon and its brilliant ray struck through the stern window to light the chart—a favourable omen perhaps, like the clear weather and fair wind which were so precisely what he needed. A less favourable omen for the future was the behaviour of Captain Clewes, whose common sense should have told him that it was desirable for the convoy to keep together; he might have expected that Clewes, with the fastest vessel in the convoy, would not be able to resist showing off. However, it was of no great moment that *Dragon* should be first at the rendezvous, providing she got there.

The chart was a Swedish one and showed the channels and land masses from Jutland in the west to Zealand in the east. The fortunate sighting of Cape Arkona on the north coast of Germany—another good omen?—gave him his present position with enough accuracy for his purpose. The course he was shaping would take the convoy across the southern approaches and into what looked on the chart to be a trap—the narrowing corner of sea between the southernmost Danish islands and the coast of Schleswig-Holstein, from whose inner end the Little Belt wormed its even more constricted way northward. Like Denmark, the Schleswig duchies were under the thumb of Bonaparte, but so far as Mr Fitton knew no warships of any size lurked in those marshy inlets, nor did he expect to encounter many trading vessels until he had passed the Fehmarn Belt. His finger, moving on the chart and tracing his course, made a shallow curve south-west and then west-nor'-west round the south coasts of sea-split eastern Denmark. The Fehmarn Belt, a strait twelve miles wide between Danish Lolland and German Fehmarn, was plain sailing with no awkward shoals; if this weather held there should be no difficulty in passing it after nightfall. Beyond it on the same course he would steer clear of the tip of the big Danish island

61

of Langeland, to turn on a short nor'-westerly leg of a dozen miles and reach the rendezvous in the Marstal Bugt. This was the area in which he hoped to bring off a *coup de main* which—he had to admit it—could not be certain of achievement but was certain to be hazardous.

The hasty planning that had been forced on him at the convoy conference would have to be adhered to because there was no other course. Here at the entrance to the seventy-mile windings of the Little Belt the Danish sea-traffic would be undiminished; this secluded corner of the Baltic was so far from the range of the British patrolling squadron that the small craft plying between its diminutive ports pursued a peace-time trade without interruption. The larger vessels no doubt carried on trade with the German ports of Flensburg and Schleswig—even, perhaps, with Lubeck—but there must be a host of little ships busy between Svendborg and Sonderborg, Hejlsminde and Assens and Middelfart, right up the Little Belt to the fortified port of Fredericia where it made its exit into an arm of the Kattegat. Every one of those little ships would have on board at least one man capable of piloting a vessel through the Little Belt. Now that the onward progress of his convoy depended on his securing such a man Mr Fitton could admit to a certain relief; the route that lay ahead of him, totally unknown except from study of the chart, was by far the most intricate piece of pilotage he had ever attempted.

One of the names that had caught his eye as he considered the chart stirred his memory: Svendborg. That, according to Clewes, was the present residence of King Christian of Denmark and his court. Here it was, at the tip of an inlet—Svendborg Sound—that branched eastward from the Little Belt entrance. In the coast ten miles south of Svendborg Sound was the large semicircular bay called the Marstal Bugt where he proposed to anchor the convoy, in nine fathoms just off the western arm of the bay, the Vejnaes Nakke. It was fortunate, reflected Mr Fitton, that the tidal range in the Baltic was so small as to be negligible; he had no tidal currents to contend with and the soundings on the chart could be regarded as unchanging. It made his plan of ambush a great deal simpler.

Someone knocked on the cabin door and a hoarse voice hailed him.

"Sir! Mr Honeyburn's compliments, an' *Dragon*'s in sight ahead."

"Very well."

Mr Fitton rolled up the chart and went on deck. *Dragon* was visible from the quarterdeck, hove-to on the brilliant blue water four miles ahead. It was some comfort that Clewes had not sailed on by himself but less comforting to have with him a man whose behaviour was unpredictable.

"Mr Sholto!"

The redheaded bos'n, who was acting as signal midshipman, hurried aft.

"Hoist *Dragon*'s number and 'Keep better station'."

It was not what he would have preferred to say but the code arranged for the convoy permitted nothing better. The blue-and-yellow squares of numeral three, *Dragon*'s code number, soared fluttering up with two alphabetical flags below them. Clewes didn't trouble himself to acknowledge, but when the gun-brig, half-an-hour later, brought her on the beam the captain could be seen waving his hat and apparently executing a sort of fandango on his quarterdeck.

"Why in heaven's name is the fellow dancing?" demanded Mr Fitton of his lieutenant.

Honeyburn coughed gently. "I heard a voice—it said 'Drink, pretty creature, drink.' "

"I suppose that's possible even at this hour. But I'm uncertain, Mr Honeyburn, whether your 'pretty creature' refers to me or to Mr Clewes."

"To *Dragon*, perhaps. She at least deserves it."

Dragon had paid off before the wind and was gathering way well out on *Cracker*'s port quarter, a sight of breathtaking beauty with the newly-risen sun right astern of her making the bellying sails seem filled with urgent light rather than with the invisible breeze. To compare her with her captain, reflected Mr Fitton, was to perceive that the works of man can be more admirable than the works of God.

His mild jest with Honeyburn had lightened his mood. Or perhaps it was the satisfaction of having all the convoy once more under his eye; like an old hen gathering the last of her brood under her wing, he thought with an inward grin. At any rate, he had made that spontaneous change of outlook which turns the better side of all things uppermost, so that he could think of Clewes as a clown instead of as a dangerous fool and concede that Henry Honeyburn, a sea-officer of incurable inefficiency, was in other ways a man of considerable intelligence. He took his watch from the fob in the waistband of his breeches and consulted it.

"There's some while yet before I relieve you on deck, Mr Honeyburn," he said, "but I don't propose to go below again. I shall be obliged if you'll walk with me for a little."

"Honoured, sir, of course."

They moved to the starboard rail and began to pace up and down the short length of the quarterdeck side by side, turning inward towards each other with short stamping steps at the end of the ten paces as time-honoured ritual required. For a minute or so they walked in silence. Cape Arkona was out of sight now and the sea horizon empty all round them. The next landfall would be the end of the Gjodser peninsula, the most southerly point of Denmark. He remarked as much to his companion and was answered with a courteous acquiescence which he found mildly irritating. It was well enough for Honeyburn to insist on his junior status, maintaining this charade of post-captain and first lieutenant between them, but his evident contentment to remain in total ignorance of his commander's future plans was less easy to bear. Mr Fitton knew that the fault was partly his; it had always been his foible to confide in no one, to let his orders in the time of action be the first revelation of his tactics. To keep Honeyburn in the dark was unjust as well as foolish and he was going to amend that. But he would have found it easier if the lieutenant had shown some curiosity.

"Mr Honeyburn," he said abruptly, "I need your advice."

"I doubt that, sir," Honeyburn said modestly. "If it's concerned with practical seamanship—"

"Perhaps I should have said your criticism. And the plan I've formed concerns strategy and tactics rather than seamanship. You must know that at yesterday's conference—"

He described how he had agreed to get hold of a Danish pilot before entering the Little Belt.

"I had no choice but to agree," he went on. "My plan, therefore, is to anchor the convoy in the Marstal Bugt while we seize some Danish fishing vessel or coaster and take from her a man to act as pilot. You've looked at the chart. Eight miles north-west of the anchorage the Svendborg Sound runs off east to Svendborg, a sizeable place by all accounts. I propose to take *Cracker* to the mouth of the sound and intercept the first vessel coming out. You may have wondered why I delayed the convoy sailing-time. It was—"

"It's plain enough now!" Honeyburn's obvious excitement excused the interruption; his pale eyes glinted and his usually rather vacant face was comically animated. "You wanted the convoy at anchor well before first light, with time enough left for capturing a prize, if possible while it's still dark. And of course you'll try for an outward-bound vessel. A boat inward-bound might be expected at Svendborg and the alarm given when she failed to arrive. How long d'you—" He checked himself in some embarrassment. "May I ask, sir, how long you

65

a

expect to take over the passage of the Little Belt—to Fredericia, let us say?"

Mr Fitton concealed surprise. "It could be two days, or even three."

"Good gracious! But of course," Honeyburn hurried on, "you'll move the convoy only at night and lie-up by day. In the lee of an island—'some secreted island, heaven knows where'—as Wordsworth has it. And a contrary wind, or lack of any, might mean we'd take a week."

By now he was so absorbed in what he was saying that he would have marched straight on for'ard had not Mr Fitton taken him by the elbow and swung him back to the quarter-deck. He gave no sign of noticing this but continued to talk, his reedy voice taking on a certain pedagoguish tone.

"The essence of your problem—our problem—is avoidance of disclosing our presence. The chart shows nothing of the roads on land but it seems to me that a horseman could ride from Svendborg to Fredericia in a day. You'd try to pass the fortress by night, unseen?"

"I see no other way."

"It's the exit from the Little Belt. Could they close it?"

"The passage is less than a mile wide there. If they had warning enough they could close it with a boom—boats linked by cables."

"Then they must have no warning." Honeyburn was thumping fist into palm in the intensity of his thinking. "That's axiomatic and there you have it. The corollary follows—the capture of your pilot must be contrived so that no one on shore knows of it for at least three days. How do you propose to effect this seizure of a Danish vessel?"

"By getting alongside and boarding her," replied Mr Fitton humbly.

Honeyburn clicked his tongue. "And if she chances to be the faster craft and wins clear, the alarm's given for certain and we'll never pass Fredericia. Fire a shot across her bows, knock her topmast down, and the result's almost as certain." He halted suddenly in the middle of their walk and Mr Fitton perforce halted also. "Mark this now, Fitton," said Mr Honeyburn, wagging a monitory finger as at a laggard pupil, "that way will not do. We must have something a deal quieter. We must—"

He checked himself there, his jaw dropping as he realised that he was treating his senior officer to a lecture. The sight of Mr Fitton's broad grin hardly reassured him and he stammered in redfaced embarrassment.

"I really—dear me! I trust, sir, you'll pardon—"

"Nonsense. I asked your advice and I still want it." Mr Fitton's hand on Honeyburn's arm started them on their quarterdeck walk again. "I fancy I should have asked it earlier. You have a suggestion to make, I'm assured. What is it that we must do?"

Thus adjured, Mr Honeyburn told him, though in a less didactic manner than before. When he had finished it was Mr Fitton's turn to stop their pacing; he set hands on hips and regarded his lieutenant with mingled admiration and puzzlement.

"It's admirable and we'll act upon it," he said. "Tell me, Mr Honeyburn—how do you come to have such a grasp of strategy?"

"Well, really, sir, I don't know." Mr Honeyburn rubbed his chin. "Unless I've imbibed it from so much teaching of Caesar's *Gallic Wars*."

For the rest of that day the convoy maintained its speed on the westward course, the wind holding steady from the east. During the afternoon two distant sail were sighted towards the coast of Germany, and a little before sunset, when they made the landfall of the Gjodser point to northward, *Cracker*'s lookout reported several small fishing-vessels cruising offshore

67

in that direction. The landfall enabled Mr Fitton to obtain a rough fix from bearing and distance and set a course to take him through the wide Fehmarn Belt in darkness. His last signal had been for the convoy to form line ahead and follow in his wake; and in the small hours of next morning, with a late-rising moon revealing the low dark outline of uninhabited coast ahead, the nine ships glided under topsails into the Marstal Bugt. Eight of them anchored in the arm of the bay. A boat from the gun-brig sped across to *Dragon* with a written message for Captain Clewes, and then *Cracker*, bracing round her topsails, moved slowly out round the Vejnaes Nakke headland and crept up the coast towards the mouth of the Svendborg Sound.

4

A cold dawn broke very slowly across the empty Danish waterways and islands, its pale light challenged by the faint golden radiance of a setting moon. Mr Fitton, muffled in his boat-cloak, shivered in the chill of the dawn wind from the east and thanked his stars that it had lost its briskness during the night. He was standing beside a rusty iron framework like a giant lobster-pot which was perched on the stony turf of the headland, almost at its narrow tip and some forty feet above the sea; the framework was a beacon, though his groping fingers could find no charred sticks beneath it to show that it had been recently used, and marked the southern gatepost (as it were) of the entrance to the Svendborg Sound. Northward he looked across the pallid waters of the sound to its farther shore three miles away, at present no more than a suggestion of darker masses spreading under the vault of the lightening sky. On his right hand the inner reaches of the sound stretched into the glimmering twilight where Svendborg lay at its head, on his left he could look steeply down on *Cracker*'s jolly-boat, a black shape lying off the muddy shore at the mouth of the Little Belt. There was not one light twinkling in the distance, not one human sound, to indicate that these coasts and islands were inhabited.

The gun-brig had been left at anchor in charge—to his evident disappointment—of Mr Honeyburn, a mile to southward and close under the lee of the headland. The chart had suggested this attenuated strip of land as a lookout post and Mr Fitton had landed from the jolly-boat to watch for a likely prize. It looked as though it would be a long watch. By the time the moon had vanished below the horizon where the Danish mainland lay invisible, he was convinced that the seafarers of these parts did their voyaging by daylight; which was after all to be expected when their ports of call were rarely more than a day's sail apart. It increased his chances of moving the convoy through the Little Belt undetected but also increased the hazards of his present enterprise. He had hoped to use Mr Honeyburn's stratagem in the half-light before sunrise, not in the broad light of morning.

Half-an-hour later the gradual increase of light revealed the shapes of low flat islands higher up the sound. With his glass he could make out windmills on the far shore, a cluster of houses here and there on the larger islands, and—at last—tiny brown sails moving from the direction of Svendborg. A grey haze was creeping over the sky from the east and the colours of the coming sunrise showed yellow instead of rose. He kept his glass on the brown sails. They had a light following wind but it was another thirty minutes before the boats were in open water and near enough for identification: fishing-boats, seven of them in close company and so of no use for his purpose.

He was already crouching below the skyline. Now he clambered down a little way on the outer side and pitched his voice to reach Sholto and his men in the jolly-boat.

"Bring her right inshore. No talking."

It was unlikely that the fishing-boats would come close enough to see the jolly-boat but he was taking no chances. They might catch sight of the gun-brig if they headed south when they were out of the Sound but there was nothing he could do about that. He returned to the crest, lying on his chest beside the beacon and resting his glass on a handy stone. Men's voices came very faintly down the wind as the brown sails approached, well out in the Sound. The fishing-fleet held straight on past the headland and soon was a flock of diminishing brown specks making westward.

The sun was up behind a grey mass of cloud when he caught the glint of white in his lens. It moved slowly out from behind the flat bank of an islet and turned for the mouth of the Sound—he could make out the flicker of the mainsail as she gybed. Cutter-rigged, then. The long minutes passed slowly as he watched her approach. No fishing-vessel, this, but a trim cutter with yellow-painted hull and some sort of coloured pendant or whip at the masthead; probably with a crew of three or four.

Mr Fitton swept his glass slowly from north to east across the waters of the Sound and saw no other sail. He turned westward. Two sail were in sight, but right on the horizon. This was his chance. He returned his gaze to the cutter, estimating her speed and watching what course she shaped. She was making, as the fishing-boats had done, for the middle of the entrance, which meant that she would pass nearly a mile out from the headland. It was time to move.

He wriggled backwards from the beacon and sprang down to the beach. Sholto had the bows of the jolly-boat close in among the big stones and he hopped nimbly into the stern-sheets.

"Mr Sholto, I'll ask you to take the bow oar now. I want Erikson in the bows. And get those cutlasses out of sight, Garroway.—Shove off. Give way, port—give way together."

The jolly-boat, with three seamen and the bos'n at the oars, slid out from the cover of the headland. As she did so Mr Fitton slid down until he was sitting on the bottom-boards with his shoulders resting on the stern thwart and pulled his boat-cloak across his body up to his neck. It was an uncomfortable position but it was possible that on so smart a craft as the cutter someone might have a telescope. By raising his head a little he could look to starboard, across the ridges of small waves luminous with the diffused morning radiance, and watch the cutter. She was about half-a-mile away on the bow and heading to cross the jolly-boat's course, her big mainsail well out to starboard to catch the quartering breeze. He raised his voice above the creak of rowlocks.

"Ready for your speech, Erikson? Make it sound urgent—we're all relying on you."

"Aye aye, sir," said Erikson from the bows. "Our ship's hard aground—injured man like to die. I'll pitch it hot and strong," he added with a grin.

"Very well. We come alongside the instant she heaves-to. You'll board when I say 'now!', Peters remaining in the boat. Look murderous and wave your cutlasses but don't use them—I don't want anyone hurt." He stole a cautious glance over the gunwale. "Pull harder. Hold water when you're dead ahead of the cutter."

He lowered his head and waited, motionless. It was Honey-burn who had reminded him that the Norwegian tongue was nearly indistinguishable from Danish and had suggested Erikson's "speech". Sholto and the four seamen could be taken for sailors of any nation in their rough and salt-stained clothing; Mr Fitton was no rich post-captain able to dress his crew in uniform colours. The boat-cloak concealed his own epauletted coat and he was using his cocked hat as a pillow.

" 'Vast pulling," he heard the bos'n mutter.

As the oarsmen obeyed and the boat's way slackened Mr Fitton slid a pistol from its place under the stern thwart and grasped it beneath his boat-cloak. Erikson stood up in the bows and raised a powerful voice.

"Aho-o-oy!"

That, at least, was a universal sea language. A brief, distant reply came to his ears; then Erikson yelled a sentence or two and was answered by a nearer shout. The ripple of water under the approaching cutter's forefoot was audible now, and gruff Danish voices in question and reply. Erikson was jabbering again, his intensely agonised tones suggesting that he fancied himself as a tragedian; but his appeal for help and dramatic gesture at the "injured man" in the sternsheets evidently gained their object. Mr Fitton heard the crackle of canvas and swirl of water as the cutter came round head-to-wind, and her yellow side slid into view a few feet above his motionless head. He had time to notice an elaborately carved badge on her bow—a lion rampant, red on a white ground—before the jolly-boat's gunwale ground against the cutter's planking.

"*Now!*" he shouted, throwing off the boat-cloak and struggling to his feet.

The cutter's rail was level with his head and it was an easy matter to swing himself over onto her deck. Sholto and the three seamen boarded almost simultaneously, the bos'n with his cutlass gripped between his teeth. Pistol in hand, Mr Fitton glanced quickly round him—and could not repress a smile at his own melodramatic attitude.

There were only three men on deck and all of them wore smart blue jackets and round caps with a ribbon at the back. At this instant they were struck motionless with astonishment, one at the tiller, another with the slack of the mainsheet in his hands, the third by the rail staring open-mouthed at Garroway's cutlass describing circles a foot or two from his head.

Mr Fitton thought of Horace's mountains that laboured and brought forth a ridiculous mouse. But it was necessary to keep up this show of violence, to convince the Danes that any resistance meant death.

"Tie 'em up!" he ordered harshly, and the two deckhands were bound hand and foot with the lashings brought for the purpose. "Erikson, come aft here."

He had sprung to the helmsman's side and was holding his cocked pistol (it was not loaded) to the man's head. The Dane, a big bearded man with the barrel chest and mighty shoulders of a swimmer, let go of the tiller and gazed at the weapon in mingled apprehension and surprise.

"Ask him who commands here," he ordered when Erikson trotted aft.

At the question, the helmsman's glance darted to the raised foredeck a little for'ard of the mast; there was a door amidships below that deck, Mr Fitton saw, with a few steps leading down to it.

"He says he's the skipper, sir," Erikson translated the mumbled reply.

"Very well. Stay here. Show him your cutlass and tell him you'll slit him open if he takes a step or makes a sound."

He strode towards the for'ard door. The cutter was just about big enough to accommodate two cabins there, and there could be other—

"*Nom de Dieu! Qu'est-ce qu'arrive là-haut?*"

A man's voice, deep and arrogant, brought him to a brief halt at the top of the short ladder. A Frenchman on board? As he went down the steps the door opened. A woman stood there, a woman small and slender in a silver-grey gown with lace at bosom and sleeves. Fair hair braided in the Danish fashion, wide brown eyes that sparkled angrily as she stared up at him—so much he noted before he recovered his self-possession and his voice.

c*

"*Retirez-vous, madame.*" He rasped the words, gesturing with his pistol. "*A l'instant!*"

"I shall do nothing of the kind!" She came forward, forcing him to draw back the muzzle of the pistol. "Who are you?"

"*Pardon,*" said Mr Fitton curtly.

He placed his hand on her breast and thrust her firmly backwards, pulling the door shut the moment she was inside. There was a brass hook and staple on the outside and he secured them and tested the fastening. It was only as he sprang up the steps to the deck that he realised that she had spoken in English.

A glance showed the waters in his immediate vicinity empty. Eastward, towards Svendborg, there was a movement of sails beyond the intervening islands.

"Jolly-boat's towing astern, sir," said Sholto, coming up. "This craft's named *Amalie*, seemingly."

"Very well. Send a hand to fore and main sheets."

Little more than five minutes after her capture the cutter *Amalie* brought the morning breeze on her beam and began to make for the lee of the headland and the waiting gun-brig, with the blue-clad Danish skipper sullenly handling the tiller. Mr Fitton, standing beside the helm with his pistol displayed, had a number of problems and puzzles to occupy his mind but was unable to concentrate on more than one: if a pair of wide brown eyes could take his breath away when they were angry, what effect would they have on him if they were kind?

FOUR

Passengers and Prisoners

I

The Marstal Bugt was something of an oddity among bays. Its oddness, which was more obvious on Mr Fitton's Swedish chart than on the spot itself, had made him choose it for an anchorage as soon as he saw it on the chart. His plan to bring off an early-morning kidnapping of a pilot meant that the convoy must remain hidden for the remainder of that day, and though he could not render eight three-masted merchant ships and a gun-brig invisible there was a chance that in the Marstal Bugt they would at least be indiscernible. On the morning of October 5th, as he rounded the Vejnaes Nakke in the cutter with *Cracker* just ahead of him, he could confirm that his choice had been a good one.

The Bugt, a semicircular indentation eight miles across, was not really a bay at all. It was the sea space between the butts of two large islands, Aero and Langeland, which—like many of the Danish islands—were separated from each other by vast areas of shoal water dotted with banks and islets, waters where no boat larger than a coble could find a passage. At the innermost curve of the Bugt, where a two-mile gap lay between the tips of the two islands, the intervening shoal lay less than three feet below the surface, so that a man might walk from

Aero to Langeland across the sea. Except at the Bugt's western arm, which ended in the minor hill above the Vejnaes Nakke headland, the shores were low, featureless, and uninhabited, and the Vejnaes Flak shoal off the mouth of the bay caused vessels making for the Little Belt to pass at least ten miles out from the Marstal shore. The sum of this was that the convoy's first anchorage in enemy waters was as safe as was possible in the circumstances. The only danger was the advent of some inshore fishing-boat which might escape and give the alarm.

The eight ships had anchored in five fathoms below the Vejnaes Nakke hill, where their topmasts did not reach to the skyline. *Cracker* and *Amalie* brought up at the outer end of the line and dropped their anchors. Mr Fitton sent the three Danish sailors in the jolly-boat to the gun-brig with Mr Sholto and two hands as armed escort, and having supervised Peters and Erikson as they lowered the cutter's sails turned his attention to the prisoners in her cabin for'ard.

On the brief southward passage down the coast he had concentrated on the immediate business of getting his two vessels into the shelter of the Marstal Bugt, sparing time only for an interrogation of the Danish skipper through Erikson. The skipper had stubbornly refused to give any information other than his name, Svane, and *Amalie*'s intended destination, which was the ancient port of Kolding. Of the prisoners in the cabin he would only say, according to Erikson, that they were "two persons of consequence, who will punish you for this". As far as it went, the information was useful. Kolding, Mr Fitton saw from the chart, lay at the head of a short fjord running west from the Little Belt four miles south of Fredericia; that made it certain that Svane was a competent pilot for the Little Belt, by daylight at any rate. And it now seemed probable that there were two people, not more, in the for'ard cabin and therefore small likelihood of resistance when he took them into custody. That the two were persons of consequence he had already inferred from *Amalie*'s appearance. The heraldic badge on the cutter's bows, the gilding on the cabin door-panels, the fine carving of the taffrail and the whiteness of her cordage, all declared that she was a pleasure-craft owned by someone of wealth and consequence; remembering whence she had sailed, he thought it not impossible that she was the property of King Christian of Denmark himself. He had chosen his prize unluckily but it was too late to amend that now.

A patch of sunlight slid across *Amalie*'s white deck as he walked aft. The mid-morning sky held channels of blue between its grey cloud-islands, and the wind, a light breeze, had backed north of east, which was not encouraging. Because of certain thumpings and bangings coming from the cabin he had posted one of the hands as sentry by the door until the cutter was at anchor, but now the man had been withdrawn and there was no sound from the cabin. The curious circumstance that the girl (or woman, for she was certainly in her thirties) spoke English while her male companion spoke French would now be explained, he reflected as he went down the steps and released the catch of the door. When he pulled it open he was confronted by a table upended across the opening and the barrel of a sporting gun resting on its edge.

"You will halt there and explain yourself," said the man behind the gun, in French.

He was of middle height, as far as could be seen, with a lean wrinkled face and iron-grey hair. Two arrogant eyes, narrowed under heavy lids, looked down a beak of a nose at his captor. Mr Fitton's French was presentable though somewhat rusty and he replied in that language.

"Your gun is unnecessary, monsieur. I am unarmed, as you see. Your vessel is a prize of war, and you—"

"A prize of war! *Nom de Dieu!*" The narrowed eyes widened and flashed. "Do you take this yacht for a warship, imbecile?

77

My gun is necessary—for duck-shooting. *Sacr-r-é!* His Majesty shall know there are pirates in his dominions! I demand—"

"*Laissez-moi, papa.*" The woman's voice was firm and clear; the elderly man and his gun withdrew, or were withdrawn, and the small woman he had seen before appeared behind the table. "He loses his temper too easily," she said in English.

Mr Fitton took off his hat and bowed. "It's the fault of many of us, madame," he said. "But not, I'm sure, of yourself."

She tilted her chin and the brown eyes flashed like her father's.

"You may spare your compliments, sir," she told him haughtily. "I await the explanation you were asked for."

It would be imprecise to call her beautiful, he was thinking. And pretty was too trivial a word. Maturity was part of the charm; and so was the direct glance from beneath level brows, the skin that was palest gold rather than white, the rounded chin. There was a dimple in the chin—and it was tilting more than ever under his gaze. Mr Fitton pulled himself together.

"Of course. My name is Michael Fitton, lieutenant in His Britannic Majesty's Navy. I need a pilot for the Little Belt. I now have your skipper, Svane, who'll be made to pilot my vessels through to the Kattegat."

"Made? You'll force him at pistol-point," she said scornfully. "As you did me."

"If necessary—but in your case, madame, I'd thought you hadn't noticed the pistol."

"Indeed I did!" she blazed at him. "And the blow you gave me when I ignored it!"

Mr Fitton reddened. "It was not," he said emphatically, "a blow. It was a push."

"It was a blow, sir! You—"

"Nonsense. A blow implies a sharp impact. I flatly deny that there was any impact. All I did was to place my hand on your—um—in short, madame, it was a push."

78

A smile quivered at the corner of her mouth. For a moment laughter sparkled in her eyes, and Mr Fitton's heart turned over. Then her father's voice spoke in angry question from behind her and her face hardened into its former defiance.

"You've taken poor Svane," she said evenly. "The yacht you can have no need of. You'll allow us to go on our way in *Amalie*."

"That's quite impossible, and you've sense enough to know why." He felt a passing wonder that he should be speaking to her as man to man. "England and Denmark are at war and *Amalie* is my prize. You and your father are prisoners of war. Unless," he added, struck with a sudden doubt, "you yourself are English?"

"I'm French," she said quickly.

"Yet you speak better English, madame, than many an Englishwoman."

She frowned. "You exaggerate. I haven't been in England for six years. I was twelve years old when my father fled there from the Terror and we lived in London for fourteen years before we returned. My mother died there."

Before she had finished speaking Mr Fitton had received sudden enlightenment. Half-heard phrases spoken by Captain Clewes rushed into his mind—*La Haye . . . Boney's good books . . . Svendborg . . . King, Baron, Baron's daughter and all*. Here under his hand were Bonaparte's representative in French-controlled Denmark and his daughter. Baron La Haye and Madame—Madame Brennier, that was it; widow of a French marshal. There was matter for consideration in this, matter that concerned England and the war—that concerned him personally, also. It could mean—

"*Que dit-il, Anne?*" called her father impatiently from the cabin.

"You may tell Monsieur le Baron what I say, Madame Brennier," Mr Fitton said quickly. "You are both prisoners of

79

war. You'll be treated courteously if you do precisely as I ask. I shall be obliged to take you aboard my own ship and I fear the quarters won't have the comforts you're accustomed to, but I'll do what I can. You have one hour from now in which to collect your belongings—and remove this barrier—before you and your father are transferred to the gun-brig."

He had expected protest, perhaps anger, but she merely gazed steadily at him, her fingertips resting on the edge of the table-top between them.

"I rely on you to be ready," he went on, "and to see that no weapons are hidden in your baggage. Monsieur le Baron's gun, and his pistols if he carries them, must be left in the cabin."

"We have little or no baggage," she told him coldly. "It was sent to Kolding by a trading vessel yesterday, with my maids."

Her maids. Of course—she was a great lady. Her father was the most powerful man in Denmark, in effect the Emperor's viceregent, and Anne Brennier would hold high rank at the court of King Christian. For some reason the reminder woke sharp resentment in him.

"You'll find no lady's maids aboard my ship, madame," he snapped.

"For your reputation's sake, sir, I'm glad to hear it," she retorted with equal sharpness.

Mr Fitton, who had been ashamed of his sneer the moment it was uttered, was further disarmed by the speed of her riposte. His resentment vanished behind a grin.

"I've no reputation, bless you," he said, "except for keeping my word. And I give you my word that if you're ready as I've requested there will be no second—um—push. *A bientôt, madame.*"

He shut the door quickly and secured the catch. The petty satisfaction of having the last word was short-lived. As soon as he turned to go aft he saw Lieutenant Honeyburn clambering on board from the jolly-boat, his bony face expressive of congratulation and curiosity. Beyond his lanky figure Mr Fitton caught sight of *Cracker*, sitting on the grey-green water with the eight three-masters like a duckling beside a flock of geese, and remembered her very limited accommodation. There were urgent problems to be resolved and swift decisions to be made—and he had been wasting time in repartee with an attractive woman.

"I beg to offer felicitations, sir," beamed Honeyburn, whirling up a hand in salute. "May I ask—"

"Later, Mr Honeyburn. Your plan, as you've seen, was successful. What have you done with the Danes?"

"Foc'sle, sir—they're safe enough with the hands and Mr Sholto's on the foredeck with a musket in case they try to swim for it."

"Very well. Attend to me, now." Mr Fitton had been thinking fast. "*Cracker*'s taking on board two more prisoners. They're both French—the Baron La Haye and his daughter Madame Anne Brennier."

Honeyburn goggled at him. "A woman? Good gracious! How on earth—"

"Listen, Honeyburn, if you please. You'll share my cabin. Yours will have to be given up to Madame Brennier. The Baron—he's her father—will have one of the midships cabins. It had better be Trapp's, and Trapp can move in with Grattan. Warn Grattan, by the way, that he'll be cooking meals for the nobility and gentry. Shorty, I mean Hezekiah Band, will serve them in my cabin—and see he washes that filthy apron he insists on wearing. Have you got that?"

"I think so. But the cabins—"

"Have 'em swept out and tidied up. No time for scrubbing." Mr Fitton hesitated. "And Honeyburn—see that your cabin's as fit for a lady as you can make it."

Honeyburn, rubbing his chin, glanced askance at him.

"A touch of domesticity," he murmured. " 'Her household motions light and free, and steps of virgin liberty—' " Here he caught his commander's eye and ended with a cough.

"Belay your poetry. You've more to do than that."

The lieutenant concentrated on memorising the orders that came at him in quick succession. Back to the gun-brig to put the changes of accommodation in hand. Across to *Dragon*; request Captain Clewes to have Captains Reuterholm and Birger brought on board his ship. Mr Fitton would join them at six bells of the afternoon watch, bringing the Danish pilot with him. This message delivered, return to *Cracker*, inspect cabins, then send jolly-boat to the cutter to pick up Mr Fitton, two seamen, and two prisoners.

"And I'll have the prisoners piped aboard," Mr Fitton concluded. "The bos'n, two seamen with muskets—see they handle 'em smartly—and yourself as officer of the watch. Is all that quite clear?"

"Ye-es. Except—I've heard this Baron La Haye is Boney's minister. If—"

"So have I. Carry on, Mr Honeyburn, if you please."

As soon as Honeyburn was into the boat and away Mr Fitton set Peters and Erikson to work making all snug on the cutter's deck. He would have to leave *Amalie* here at anchor for the Danes to find later on, but to leave her other than shipshape was something he could not do. And now, as he had hoped, he had a little time in which to think. Pacing up and down the deck—but keeping well clear of the for'ard cabin— he considered the momentous circumstance which had been kept at the back of his mind for the past twenty minutes.

He had made a most important capture. *They say Christian would have second thoughts about his alliance with the French if La Haye wasn't there to keep him up to scratch.* Clewes might be wrong. But even if he was, La Haye was still the Emperor's proxy in Denmark. His capture by a British gun-brig far inside Danish territory would make a tremendous stir in England—throughout Europe, too. The man who commanded that brig could count on fame, honours, and certain promotion. Lieutenant Michael Fitton, at forty-six, would at long last receive the rewards he had almost ceased to covet. And all he had to do, now, was to bring his Baltic convoy safe through the Little Belt and home.

It was a tremendous prospect; a golden future, and the means to achieve it in his grasp. All the more curious, then, that his thoughts refused to dwell on it for long. Mr Fitton found it impossible to rid himself of a memory of brown eyes that laughed and red lips that quivered in a smile. He was still thinking of Anne Brennier when he saw the jolly-boat pulling towards the cutter.

2

Mr Sholto's silver call shrilled as the Baron La Haye, impressive in a green shooting-coat and cockaded hat, stepped over the rail onto *Cracker*'s quarterdeck. The two seamen made a creditable show of presenting their muskets. Lieutenant Honeyburn came forward hat in hand to assist Madame Brennier on board. It was well enough, decided Mr Fitton, throwing a swift glance round the orderly deck and neatly-flemished cordage as he followed; this was a King's ship, small as she was, and the distinguished prisoners would be aware of the discipline and authority she lived by. He had been at some pains to preserve a strictly formal manner during the business of embarking in the jolly-boat, and there had been no conversation on the short boat passage. He maintained that distant coldness now.

"Lieutenant Honeyburn will conduct you to your quarters, madame," he said; and in French, "Monsieur le Baron, oblige me by following Mr Sholto—I regret that I cannot accommodate you in adjoining cabins. One of these men—" he indicated the temporary musketeers—"will be posted outside each cabin. If you require anything please let them know and they will inform Mr Honeyburn."

He touched his hat stiffly and was about to turn away when Anne's voice recalled him.

"By your leave, sir—there's something we shall require quite soon, I fear—food. You remember? Your morning call disturbed our *petit déjeuner*."

Mr Fitton had not forgotten the matter of food but he had omitted to mention it. He concealed his annoyance behind an impassive countenance.

"I shall dine in my cabin, madame," he informed her with dignity, "and I trust to be honoured with the company of yourself and Monsieur le Baron. That will be at one bell of the first dogwatch."

He touched his hat again and walked quickly away before she could ask what time that was. Honeyburn would tell her. Let her ask him. Beside the forehatch Garroway was on guard, heels together and musket tucked up against shoulder in imitation of the marine regiment; his weatherbeaten face wore a faint grin, presumably at his own unaccustomed pose.

"Take that smirk off your face or I'll flog it off," snapped Mr Fitton viciously.

As he went down the ladder he was wondering irritably what had happened to his wonted imperturbability, the philosophic calm which (he had thought) middle age had stamped finally and permanently on his attitude to life. Down in the narrow mess-deck the three Danish prisoners were sitting with half-a-dozen of the hands in noisy conclave and he caught a brief glimpse of a pair of dice being swept out of sight before the men stood up at his entrance. He nodded and passed on to the galley, where Grattan the cook squatted in the gloom with his bulbous nose in the pages of a tattered book.

"There'll be four persons dining in my cabin," Mr Fitton told him. "What's that you're reading, Mr Grattan?"

Grattan, a slow-speaking Ulsterman, straightened himself and held out the book so that he could see the title on its dirty cover: *The Art of Cookery made Plain and Easy*, by Mrs Hannah Glasse.

" 'Tis a syllabub I was thinking of, sor," he said. "If I had but a pint of the Madeira wine—"

"No," said Mr Fitton firmly. "I'll have no syllabubs, Mr Grattan, and you may put Mrs Glasse overside. Pea soup— your best—followed by the boiled salt-beef tongue with pickled cabbage. Put a dozen pippins out of the barrel on a clean dish, and see that every apple's sound."

"Aye aye, sir." The cook looked disappointed. "By what Mr Honeyburn said consarning nobility and gentry I'd thought you'd be wanting something special."

"Do as I've said and be sure the hot dishes are hot. That's what I want." He went out of the galley and then put his head in again. "You need cream for a syllabub, so far as I remember. Where did you propose to get cream?"

Grattan scratched his head. " 'Twas my idea, sor, to mix up a touch of flour and water for the cream."

"You may thank the saints you didn't make that syllabub, Mr Grattan," said Mr Fitton.

On deck again he felt his temper somewhat restored. The Baron and his daughter were out of sight, the bos'n with a party of six hands was overhauling the spare cable on the foredeck, and Honeyburn was supervising another party who were greasing the trunnions of the after carronades. *Cracker* had at least the outward appearance of normality and he found this soothing. It was possible to brush aside the gaudy vision of Post-Captain Fitton, wealthy and famous, restorer of the fallen greatness of the Fittons, and—for a moment at least—be content with the command of a gun-brig.

"There's no need to stand like a Tussaud waxwork," he said to Garroway, who was still rigid at the forehatch. "Shoulder your musket and walk about—and keep an eye on the man up yonder."

The man could be seen as a slow-moving figure on the undulating skyline of the coast three-quarters of a mile away. The message Mr Fitton had sent to *Dragon* early that morning had included a request that Clewes would put a lookout on shore to give warning if anyone approached from the landward side or if a vessel of any size appeared to be heading in for the Marstal Bugt from westward. Not that the convoy or its escort could do much about it in either case, Mr Fitton reflected; the fellow needn't make himself quite so conspicuous on the skyline—but after all there was small likelihood of a Danish ship coming close enough to see him.

He looked across the empty sea to west and south, where the Danish mainland and the coast of Germany lay invisible below the horizon. The sea was calm and the horizon blurred with haze. Here in the lee of the Vejnaes Nakke point it was difficult to gauge wind direction but such movement as there was in the cloud mass overhead seemed to be from the north. That was bad. A backing wind was bad in any case, but a north wind meant that the convoy would be forced to tack up the first reach of the Little Belt; it was small comfort to recall that this forty-mile reach, giving a straight course nor'west by north except at one point, averaged four miles across from shore to shore. He had better take another look at the chart.

Mr Honeyburn straightened up as his commander approached the carronade he was inspecting, but Mr Fitton nodded briefly and passed on. In the tiny alleyway at the foot of the ladder leading to the after cabins a dark figure startled him—a seaman with a musket. It was a moment or two before he remembered that this was a sentry and that Anne Brennier was in the cabin next to his. Honeyburn, he saw as he opened the door of his own cabin, had bundled his clothes and few belongings in a boat-cloak, neatly enough lashed, and stowed the bundle in a corner of the bulkhead where Mr Fitton's sword, tarpaulin coat, and cloak were hanging. It would do there for the present. For the meal this evening he could pull his sea-chest forward for one seat, and with this chair and the one from Honeyburn's cabin, and a stool from the warrant officers' mess—

Mr Fitton stopped short in his planning. It was a hazardous night voyage through the shoals he should be considering, not a supper party. He got the chart and took it to the meagre light of the stern window.

A careful measurement of the convoluted channels he would have to follow had given him a total distance of just over seventy miles to be sailed before he was out of the narrows and past Fredericia, heading through comparatively safe waters for the Kattegat. In the ten hours of darkness he could count on he could have covered all that distance—in the open sea, with a fresh breeze steady on his quarter. In the Little Belt, as he was beginning to realise, he would be fortunate if he got the convoy through with only two more nights spent on the way. The wind, falling and unfavourable as it was now, made it virtually impossible that he should get farther than the Toro Bank before dawn tomorrow. That would indeed be half the passage done, but it was by far the easier half. Immediately north of the Toro was the ten-mile section where the channel narrowed to a quarter-mile width, a long curve rounding the shoals off the islands of Aaro and Baago, and it was likely—

He lifted his head, keeping a finger on the chart. From the cabin next door came a low sweet voice singing words that he knew.

> *It was a lover and his lass*
> *With a hey and a ho and a hey nonny-no,*
> *That o'er the green cornfield did pass—*

Mr Fitton shut his ears and scowled at the chart. That channel, the Baago Sound, would be tricky by night; he would have to trust a good deal to the Danish skipper, Svane. And it was unlikely, to say the least, that the last and worst part of the route, the four bends that ended below the fortress of Fredericia, could be passed that same night. He would have to anchor again before attempting it. There might be concealment for the convoy in this eastern inlet, the Gamborg Fjord—

> *And therefore take the present time*
> *With a hey and a ho and a hey nonny-no,*
> *For love is crownéd with the prime—*

God damn it all! (Mr Fitton, rare in his generation, very seldom swore.) It was impossible to concentrate, even on matters of life and death. She must know he was in here—she couldn't fail to hear him enter. She was deliberately singing at him. Against his will he was pleased at the thought and that doubled his anger. He lugged out his watch, saw that it wanted half-an-hour before he was due to board *Dragon*, and left the cabin, shutting the door as loudly as he could without actually slamming it.

"Mr Honeyburn! I'll trouble you to have the jolly-boat manned. Mr Sholto! I want Svane—the Danish skipper—aft here. And send Erikson aft."

In less than five minutes he was being pulled across the green still water to Clewes's ship, with Svane and Erikson beside him in the sternsheets. The skipper's bearded face showed neither animosity nor cheerfulness and he sat quietly enough, but Erikson kept a hand on his wrist to discourage any attempt to swim ashore. Clewes came to *Dragon*'s rail as Mr Fitton stepped on board.

"Before your time, hey?" was his greeting. "That's the Danish bastard, is it? Why ain't he in irons? We'll have him overboard and ashore if he's loose, Fitton. I'll wager he can swim like a bloody herring."

Mr Fitton drew back involuntarily from the brandy-laden breath. "Erikson will take him below to your foc'sle until he's wanted. The Swedish captains haven't arrived?"

"Not yet—and I want to know about the skirt I saw boarding your ship." Clewes grasped his arm, leering at him. "No secrets from me, Fitton—who is she?"

Mr Fitton concealed his repugnance. "If you'll walk, sir, I'll tell you."

The brandy fumes being somewhat diffused in the up-and-down pacing, he was able to give his account in reasonable comfort.

"But damn my eyes, man!" Clewes exclaimed when he had finished. "You've got a fortune on board!—La Haye would fetch a fine ransom—or pay to be put—" He stopped, apparently overcome by a fit of coughing. "Anyway," he resumed, "you can't coop a lady up in that tub of yours. I've a spare cabin here and a bloody good one." He winked. "She won't be the first woman to occupy it. Bring her—"

"I'm obliged to you, Mr Clewes," interrupted Mr Fitton stiffly, "but I shall have to decline. Baron La Haye and Madame Brennier are prisoners of war and as such must remain in the custody of a King's officer."

Clewes shrugged and turned away. "Oh, well—I've room for 'em both if you change your mind.—There's a boat putting off from *Ahund Jakob*. Looks as if old Reuterholm's impatient to give your pilot a good going-over."

In *Dragon*'s luxurious stern cabin twenty minutes later Mr Fitton had to sit for a considerable time listening to a farrago, explosive at times, composed of three Scandinavian languages. As far as he could gather from the interchanges between Svane and Captain Reuterholm with Erikson assisting, the tongues of Denmark, Norway and Sweden were basically similar but had marked differences in the usage of certain words. The resulting arguments prolonged the examination and exacerbated the Swedish captain's temper. At length, however, Clewes was able to report that Reuterholm and Birger were satisfied that Svane was capable of piloting a vessel through the Little Belt by night, though not that he would refrain from running his captors aground if he got the chance.

"Reuterholm's promised to gut Svane like a herring if he touches a shoal," Clewes added, "but the old man still thinks he might play tricks."

"If I might say a word, sir, begging pardon," Erikson put in, "this Svane's mighty fond of the lady—devoted, like. I got that from yarning with him. I reckon he'd be more in fear for her than for himself, if you understand me, sir."

Mr Fitton considered a moment. "Tell him Madame Brennier's life will be forfeit if he runs us aground."

"I'll make it stronger than that," Clewes said with an unpleasant grin, and turned to Svane.

Whatever he said, the Swedish words evidently conveyed his meaning. The Dane's startled glance at Mr Fitton held both fear and anger and his rapid reply sounded desperate. Clewes exchanged a word or two with Captain Reuterholm and nodded.

"Svane don't like that. He'll keep clear of shoals, devil doubt him."

It was unspeakably distasteful, Mr Fitton found, to use Anne Brennier in this way; but he had to admit the necessity of binding the Danish pilot to faithful performance of his task by any method that offered itself. Erikson and Svane were dismissed from the cabin and the four men proceeded to the final arrangements for the coming night. The convoy would up anchor at *Cracker*'s signal as before, and follow in line in their present order at anchor, keeping a cable's length between ships and tacking in turn as the leader tacked. The only light allowed would be the lantern on the gun-brig's stern until two lights, one at each end of her mainyard, gave the order to anchor. Over the chart Mr Fitton pointed out the possible anchorage behind the Toro Bank, a shoal with a depth of two fathoms surrounded by deeper channels, and this was agreed upon after Clewes's objections had been overruled.

"The bloody place is only five miles south of Assens," Clewes remonstrated. "That may be only a small town—I don't doubt it's too small to have guns or a garrison—but it's a port. Any damned little skiff nosing round those channels is bound to spot nine ships lying there."

"You know a place more good, maybe?" demanded Captain Birger drily.

Mr Fitton leaned forward impatiently. "There's no alternative. If we anchor below the height—Sonderby Klint, here—we're in no worse situation than we are now."

This was translated to Reuterholm, who agreed. Clewes was overruled. All the same, Mr Fitton could sympathise with his contention, expressed when the Swedish captains had left to return on board their ships, that to sail boldly through in daylight, taking their chance in the inevitable bombardment at Fredericia, would be little more dangerous than the present plan of groping their way at night and lurking on an open coast by day. Indeed, with a steady wind from the south he would have been much inclined to take that other course. But as the jolly-boat pulled back to *Cracker* the fitful northerly breeze confirmed its present impossibility; the slightest backing towards the west could make it a headwind for tonight's passage, with the consequent uncertainty of reaching even as far as the Toro Bank before daybreak.

It was an odd sensation to set aside his concern for the safety of eight ships and their valuable cargo and consider instead the arrangements for a dinner party.

3

"*Assez bien, monsieur,*" grunted the Baron La Haye ungraciously, scowling at the glass in his hand.

It had taken three glasses of Madeira to loosen his tongue to that extent, in answer to a polite inquiry from his host. From the moment the four of them sat down at the little table in his cabin Mr Fitton suspected that La Haye had only been persuaded to eat with his captors by Anne's persistence: the choleric nobleman in *Amalie*'s cabin had become a haughty gentleman whose icy reserve yielded only the minimum of response to the conversational attempts of his enemies. It was natural enough, perhaps, in an Imperial ambassador suddenly deprived of friends and comforts and faced with the certain prospect of exile.

Though it was not yet six o'clock the overcast evening outside made it necessary to eat by lamplight, and the warm glow combined with the close quarters at which the diners were forced to sit to give an air of intimacy to the dinner-party. Anne Brennier was talking animatedly with Honeyburn (whose unexpected sociability revealed yet another hidden talent) and eating an English pippin with obvious relish, while Mr Fitton, having supervised Shorty Band in the removal of used platters, mustered his creaky French in one-sided conversation with her father. It was clear enough that the Baron understood every word of English that was spoken though he refused to respond when he himself was addressed in that language.

Madame Brennier still wore the silver-grey gown trimmed with lace, but she had placed a thin gold chain round her neck and made some indefinable change in her coiffure which to Mr Fitton's eye made her even more attractive. She seemed to accept her situation with perfect equanimity. Neither the pea soup—excellent by any standard—nor the less admirable but quite edible salt-beef tongue had tempted the Baron from his stiff and chilly silence; but Anne behaved exactly as if she had been invited to an impromptu meal in a friend's house, complimenting her host on his cook, laughing (but only after his departure) at Hezekiah Band, and discovering in Mr Honeyburn a fellow-enthusiast for the works of William Wordsworth—she had had the latest English books smuggled out to her by way of Gothenburg, it appeared. Mr Fitton could not sufficiently admire her philosophical attitude. Epictetus, he felt, would have suspended his general disapproval of women if he had known Anne Brennier.

It was becoming evident that Mr Honeyburn had taken rather more wine than was wise, and that this had revived in him the schoolmaster's resistless loquacity. The Baron's scrutiny of his wine drew his attention and he was away, careless whether or not he was understood.

"A fortified wine, sir, of course. Among your wines of France you have similar beverages. The Portuguese, however—or those of that nation who live on Madeira island—prepare their Madeira wine by methods markedly different from the French."

"*Comment?*" interjected the Baron coldly.

"We distinguish three sorts of Madeira wine—*Bual*, *Verdelho*, and *Malvasia*." Honeyburn lectured on, undeterred. "And for each we discern three stages. First a normal fermentation—"

Anne caught Mr Fitton's eye and smiled.

"He has captured Monsieur le Baron's attention," she said

93

in a low voice. "You observe it? Wine is one of my father's favourite subjects."

"It seems to be one of Honeyburn's too. Frankly, madame, I'd no idea of Honeyburn's capabilities until this evening."

"He has a great admiration for yours, sir. He's perfectly assured you'll lead this convoy fleet—eight ships, are there not?—safely through the Little Belt."

"And you, madame, are not so assured."

"My father thinks it impossible that you should succeed. For myself, I'm not sufficiently acquainted with the hazards." She glanced at him under long lashes. "Or with your capabilities, sir."

Her lashes were dark, in odd contrast with her fair hair. And if her small nose was just a trifle uptilted that was only another of the things that made her so attractive, so—

"I'm truly sorry, madame," said Mr Fitton hastily, "that you should suffer so much inconvenience by what was after all the merest chance. I fancy Monsieur le Baron and yourself were *en route* for Kolding?"

It was to have been an informal visit to Count Guldberg at the castle of Koldinghus, she told him, primarily so that her father and the Count might shoot duck together. King Christian had lent his French adviser his own yacht for the short voyage.

"And *Amalie*'s armament, as you saw," she added, "was just one gun for duck-shooting. Your cannon won't find any warships to fire on in the Little Belt, sir. The war has hardly touched the lands of Fyn and Jutland."

"Yet your father thinks we shall be opposed and captured."

Anne regarded him steadily for a moment, white teeth compressing lower lip in indecision.

"But of course," she said at last, "it's impossible that you don't know about Fredericia. No ship can pass the guns of the

94

fortress there. You'll have to surrender, you and all the others
—or be sunk by gunfire."

If his prisoners could be reasonably sure of being rescued,
reflected Mr Fitton, it went far to explain their present
unconcern.

"So you do, in fact, agree with Monsieur le Baron," he said.
"You believe that we can't get through."

She shook her head. "I believe you'll try—and I will say no
more than that."

Honeyburn's reedy voice uplifted in declamation distracted
Mr Fitton's attention. The lieutenant's discourse on wine
seemed to have turned into a literary dissertation; the Baron
might conceivably be interested in the origins of Madeira
wine, but not in the English poets.

"And if you should succeed," Anne Brennier was saying,
"what of your humble captives, sir? Where will you take us?"

"To England, naturally," said Mr Fitton; he forced himself
not to sound apologetic. "I need hardly say that the Baron
La Haye and his daughter will receive the treatment due to
persons of rank. I should think they'll send you to London—
and you'll travel a deal more comfortably than you're doing
now. You'll be prisoners, but with far more liberty and
comfort than I can give you on board *Cracker*."

"We put you to much trouble, I fear." Her tone was half
serious, half ironical. "Consider, sir, how much less compli-
cated the future would be—for us and for you—if you
contented yourself with Svane for a pilot and put the rest of
your prisoners ashore."

"I regret, madame, but that's quite impossible. The capture
of Monsieur le Baron is of great importance to my country."

"To the career of Lieutenant Fitton also, perhaps."

"Perhaps," he replied without expression. "Your glass is
empty. Pray allow me to—"

"No, please." She stopped herself; her smile held no trace

of bitterness. "You see? That should have been 'no, thank you.' My English is by no means perfect. The Madeira is very nice but it would spoil the memory of my English apple. Tell me, sir—where is your home in England?"

Mr Fitton had a fleeting vision of old Darley's hovel, where he had lived with Mary. Last time he had seen the place— when he had journeyed to Cheshire to visit Mary's grave—it had been a rubble of stones beneath the woodlands of Gawsworth Hall, once the home of his family.

"This vessel's my home, madame," he said shortly. "I've no place of my own ashore."

"No wife, then? No children?"

"My wife is dead. I've one child, a boy ten years old, living with his grandparents."

"Oh, but your home is where your son is," she cried with shining eyes. "A family is home. You know, perhaps, that my husband is dead, killed in the Spanish war. I have no child and I envy you. There is always, for you, the love that—"

"*Assez, monsieur! C'est insupportable!*"

The sharp interruption came from the Baron, who was glaring across the table at Honeyburn. Mr Fitton could cheerfully have strangled both of them; the moment of intimacy with Anne, strangely sweet to him, had gone for ever.

"What's all this, Mr Honeyburn?" he demanded.

Honeyburn looked flustered. "Well, really, sir," he stammered, "I was only citing Wordsworth's lines referring to Bonaparte. Madame Brennier will know them—'Still have I found, where Tyranny prevails'—"

"That'll do," Mr Fitton said sharply. "Monsieur le Baron's our guest and the Emperor's servant. Remembering that, you may feel you owe him an apology."

The crestfallen Honeyburn stammered a few apologetic words which the Baron received without comment or change of expression. Mr Fitton hastened to change the subject.

"We've little more time, Honeyburn, and you'll recall that we have a proposal to make to Monsieur le Baron and Madame Brennier. I shall make it now and I'd like your attention."

It was necessary that a commissioned officer should be witness to the proposal and its reply, in case of some future court of inquiry. He addressed La Haye, speaking slowly and distinctly.

"Monsieur, I wish to spare you and Madame the inconvenience of close confinement. I wish also to release for duty the two seamen who stand sentry at the doors of your cabins. This can be done very simply. You have only to give me your *paroles d'honneur* that you will make no attempt to escape from this vessel or to attract the notice of people ashore."

Presumably in deference to her father's stubborn pretence of not understanding English, Anne quickly translated this into French for his benefit. There was a rapid interchange between them, from which Mr Fitton gathered that the Baron was talked out of his first declaration that he would accept no favours from enemies.

"We give you our paroles, sir," Anne said. "And I will add my thanks."

"No need for thanks, madame. But you'll forgive me—" Mr Fitton turned to La Haye—"Monsieur le Baron is required to give his parole personally."

Again Anne translated, and the Baron, looking daggers, complied in a growl.

"*Je vous donne ma parole.*"

Mr Fitton nodded at Honeyburn and Honeyburn nodded back. Provided that one of them was alive to witness to the paroles, the other would escape the worst penalties of a court martial should either of the prisoners escape.

"And there we are," said Mr Fitton lightly. "I apologise for ending so pleasant an evening in so formal a manner. But end it must, I'm afraid." He stood up. "We have to get under way in half-an-hour. Mr Honeyburn, I'll thank you to dismiss the sentries and accompany Monsieur le Baron to his quarters. Madame—*attention!*"

The last word was a bellow. It arrested the Baron, who was about to draw himself to his full height, an instant before his head touched the low deckhead. His dignity visibly shaken, La Haye ducked out through the doorway with Honeyburn behind him. Mr Fitton, turning, surprised the flicker of a smile on Anne's face.

"I've knocked my head against that beam more than once," he explained.

"I wouldn't have thought you tall enough, sir," she rallied him.

"Haven't you heard of a man getting above himself? I sometimes do—and then I knock my head."

She laughed and gave him her hand. "At least I shan't knock mine. But I don't think there's room enough for a proper curtsey, so—I thank you, sir, for supper and your courtesy to your prisoners."

Mr Fitton essayed a bow. Since he still held Anne's hand the bow brought his lips very close to it. He kissed it. She withdrew her hand gently and preceded him from the cabin, to all appearance neither pleased nor offended by this undoubted liberty. As Mr Fitton followed, however, he knocked his head against the beam.

FIVE

The Little Belt

I

Under the long black loom of the coast the rank of ships had
melted into the fading glimmer of twilight. Two yellow sparks
climbed slowly to the masthead of the smallest ship, at the end
of the line, and at once the little fleet seemed to come to life.
A stir of noise and movement, confused yet separable into its
different sources, drifted across the scarcely rippled waters of
the Marstal Bugt; men's voices, the rustle of canvas as topsails
were unfurled from the yards, a clanking of capstan pawls, the
glint of broken water as the anchors were hove in. The two
lights sank deckward and were extinguished, to be replaced by
a single light lower down at the gun-brig's stern. Very slowly
the rank of ships began to move out from the anchorage,
following the yellow gleam at their head.

"I'll have those lee braces trimmed, Mr Honeyburn, if you
please," said Mr Fitton, peering up at *Cracker*'s topsails.

Honeyburn, standing amidships, repeated the order. Both of
them instinctively kept their voices low, though it was im-
probable that the sound would reach even as far as the shore
on their starboard hand; so quiet was the evening that the
gurgle of water under the gun-brig's slow-moving forefoot and
the faint rustle of sails scarcely filled with the gentle breeze

99

came to the ear as loud noises. The northerly airs were fitful, sometimes dropping away altogether, but this was largely due to the lee given by the Vejnaes Nakke headland. The nine vessels, irregularly spaced in line ahead, were making less than three knots through the water as they crept south-westward towards the wide entrance of the Little Belt.

Erikson was at the wheel, with the big Danish skipper standing with folded arms a little behind him. There was no need for Svane's guidance until they had turned northward into the Belt and even then there were a dozen or more sea-miles of plain sailing before the first tricky shoals were reached. Svane could take the helm before then, but Erikson would have to stay by him; it was a nuisance having to talk to a helmsman through an interpreter.

"Ask Svane which side of the Lillegrund he'll pass," Mr Fitton said to Erikson.

It was as well to let the Dane know that his captors were not entirely ignorant of the course. Erikson asked his question and received a brief reply.

"He'll pass it to east'd, sir, he says, an' steer nor'-west a league beyond."

If the Swedish chart was correct—and so far no inaccuracies had revealed themselves—that was precisely the course. The Lillegrund was a two-fathom bank in the middle of the channel south of the Toro, with a smaller shoal two miles north of it; the channel on the west was dangerously narrow, while on the east it would be necessary to hold on northward for three miles in order to clear the lesser shoal. Svane had given proof of his knowledge with his answer—though indeed that was unnecessary. As skipper of a royal yacht heading for Kolding near the farther end of the Little Belt it would have been odd if he hadn't been an expert pilot for these waters. The only uncertainty was whether he could use his knowledge by night. Mr Fitton felt reasonably sure that the threat of reprisals on the Baron and his daughter had removed any danger of treachery on the part of the skipper. He brushed that thought aside hurriedly because it brought Anne into his mind and seriously interfered with his attention to duty.

The last reflection of daylight had gone now but it was not totally dark. Overhead the stars were obscured by a drift of low cloud which before long would become luminous with moonlight, and the Vejnaes Nakke two miles away on the starboard beam was visible as the tip of a black bar gradually sliding backwards on the dark surface of the water. As *Cracker* drew out from the lee of the land her topsails filled and she lay over slightly to port, with her hull responding to a new motion through small steep waves. Four knots or thereabouts, thought Mr Fitton, and within a point of north. He glanced astern to where the eight ships of the convoy showed dark shapes on the paler darkness of the sea, a ragged line-ahead by naval standards but near enough to his own course to suffice for this first and comparatively safe passage. They were all under topsails only, like *Cracker*, and he decided to make no more sail though it meant a slow beat north-westward all night long.

"Steer west-nor'-west, quartermaster, if she'll take it," he ordered.

"Course west-nor'-west, sir."

The gun-brig brought the breeze on her bow. Honeyburn, for'ard along the deck, had the watch hauling on the braces to trim the topsails; Honeyburn would make a sea-officer yet.

"Hand over to Svane now, Erikson. You'll have to stand by all through this passage to transmit orders. You can have double watch-below when we're at anchor."

"Aye aye, sir."

The Vejnaes Nakke was lost in the night astern and *Cracker* and her train of ships might have been in the middle of the Atlantic for all that could be seen of their surroundings. Mr Fitton, with the chart a clear picture in his mind, knew that she was entering a channel six miles across from shore to shore and twenty miles long up to the twisting narrows north of the Toro Bank. The convoy, with a foul wind for its course, would have to make long reaches towards the west shore and short tacks towards the east; it would be a good three hours before they came near the Lillegrund shoal. He called Honeyburn aft.

"You'll take the deck until midnight, Mr Honeyburn, if you please. Svane has the helm and we'll go about as he directs."

"Aye aye, sir."

Honeyburn sounded subdued, perhaps because of the after-effects of the Madeira.

"When we get a moon behind these clouds you'll be able to make out the shores as we approach on each tack. If Svane takes her closer than a mile's distance put her about yourself."

"Aye aye, sir," said Honeyburn dubiously, cocking his head at the sky. " 'With how sad steps, O moon, thou climb'st the sky' ", he added in an undertone.

"Well, never mind that now," said Mr Fitton. "I shall turn in. Call me at eight bells of the middle watch. And I'd suggest you bring a hand aft to keep an eye on the stern lantern."

He did not go below immediately, however. Buttoning his pea-jacket to the neck, for the northerly breeze was chilly, he paced up and down waiting for the first tack. Odd to think that on either hand were wide territories where Bonaparte was master, where the men (or such of them as had been left by the Imperial army drafts) were bound to use every means in their power to capture or sink the convoy he was leading through the very heart of their country. Luck had been with him so far; even this wind, foul though it was, allowed him to make the progress he needed. But if the wind held from the north the convoy could not possibly get through the miles of twisting channels north of Toro, for they were too narrow to admit of even short tacks by vessels of the size and draught he was convoying. Well, that problem could be tackled when it arose. The one thing that could put paid to his enterprise no matter how fortunate he might be with winds and shoals was the alerting of Fredericia. At all costs he must keep the convoy's approach secret until it was near enough for the final dash past the unprepared guns of the fortress.

Svane growled a sentence in Danish.

"He says stand by to go about, sir," Erikson said apologetically to Mr Honeyburn.

"Very well.—Stand by to go about!" shouted Honeyburn. "Handle those braces smartly!"

The skipper put the wheel over smoothly and *Cracker* came round with the wind on her port bow. Looking into the darkness Mr Fitton watched *Dragon*, who was next astern, make the turn as she reached the faintly luminous swirl left by the gun-brig and follow in her wake. Satisfied, he went down to his cabin and lay fully dressed on his cot. He was tired; but he had not come there to sleep. Now, and only now, did he lower the mental barrier that had kept the thought of Anne Brennier from distracting him from his duty.

A score of vivid memories assailed him in an instant—her voice, the gleam of lamplight on her hair, the laughter in her brown eyes, the touch of her hand. She hadn't been displeased when he kissed her hand. She had been ready to talk intimately with him as if they had known each other for years, as if she had conceived a definite liking for him. And as far as he was concerned the feeling was something more than a liking. It was—

Mr Fitton uttered a laugh that was more like a bark. He sat up, angrily tearing open the neck of his pea-jacket, and tried to reduce his thoughts to something like order. What in heaven's name had happened to him, that he could let wild fancies trample his better judgement out of sight? He was a man of forty-six, of middle age—past middle age, some people would say—and here he was indulging in vanities like those of a coxcomb of seventeen. Moreover, he was a naval lieutenant obscure and forgotten, and Anne Brennier was a great lady, friend of royalty and widow of a marshal of France; it was totally inconceivable that they should meet even as acquaintances in any circumstances but those which, most improbably, had brought them together on board *Cracker*. Since she had courage, of course Madame Brennier had put a brave face on those circumstances. Her gaiety, her friendliness, were no more than a mask to hide her natural anxieties for the future, and her flattering attention to himself merely showed a prudent desire to keep on the right side of her captor.

He knew, as he put these propositions to himself, that the evidence of his senses was against them. But even if he could believe them true it could make no difference to his own feelings, because these were beyond the reach of reason— beyond the range of belief, he told himself exasperatedly. He had set eyes on Anne Brennier for the first time just twelve hours ago. It was not credible that in that short space of time Michael Fitton the self-sufficient, the Stoic, scorner of fools and disdainer of ambition, should have fallen in love with the woman. For that was what it amounted to, and it was absurd. He could concede that a man might look on a woman as briefly as he had looked upon Anne and feel admiration for her beauty or lust for her body, but not that he should jump unquestioning to the conclusion there was in all the world no woman for him but this one. Love at first sight? That was for boys, and a boy's love was not a man's love. So he was a fool— and it was Rochefoucauld who had said "Old fools are bigger fools than young fools".

It is one thing to admit oneself a fool, quite another to rid oneself of folly. Mr Fitton, lying down again in quest of sleep, had this obvious truth driven into him forcibly when he became aware of a rhythmic creaking on the other side of the cabin bulkhead. Honeyburn's cot always produced that

creaking when Honeyburn was lying on it and *Cracker* was reaching on the port tack, as she was now. But it was Anne who was lying on it, a few feet away, almost within arm's length of him. His vain attempts at reasoned thinking fled away like spray wind-blown from the crest of a breaker. Why, after all, was he struggling against his feelings? He was a man, Anne was a woman. He was no infatuated youngster, nor was he so inexperienced as not to know when a woman was attracted by him. His present situation, in command of the vessel that was taking the Baron La Haye and Madame Brennier to England as prisoners, might forbid his attempting anything like a courtship—such a thing, indeed, could result in his discharge from the Navy—but that situation was only temporary. Whatever the authorities in England decided to do with the Baron, his daughter would hardly be deprived of her freedom. She might well be in need of help, though, and protection, and perhaps then—

He lost himself in a succession of rosy fantasies which against all expectation ended in a dreamless sleep.

2

The *Enchiridion* of Epictetus, upon which Mr Fitton had long ago come to rely for moral guidance, enjoins that the aspiring Stoic shall prescribe to himself "some character and form of behaviour which may be preserved both alone and in company." Pacing *Cracker's* deck in the cold darkness of early morning, he perceived uneasily how far he had strayed from this prescription and how likely it was that his straying would endanger the success of his present mission. By the time the middle watch was nearly at an end he had regained his ability to concentrate all his thoughts on his convoy and its situation; which, indeed, was demanding urgent consideration.

105

D*

He had taken over the deck from Honeyburn at eight bells to find the gun-brig and her convoy on the port tack and making very little way through the almost unrippled water. The roof of cloud seemed lower overhead, but though the moon was not itself visible its light irradiated the vapour and revealed the black hump of the land right ahead. The Sonderhjorne cape, Honeyburn had reported, quoting Svane; that landfall was only slightly later than he had estimated. But when Honeyburn had gone below and Svane's word had been given to go about he saw that progress was not going to conform to his plan. Neatly handled, *Cracker* came slowly round under her topsails. But as he watched the three-masters turning in her wake he saw how narrowly each escaped being held in stays through lack of way. A cast of the log revealed a speed of hardly more than one knot. At this rate it would be full daylight before the convoy reached that dubious hiding-place behind the Toro Bank.

The gun-brig's lower courses were unfurled. There was light enough for the ship astern to see the leader's action and the other vessels followed suit. Under mainsails and topsails now, the convoy made a three-mile reach towards the western shore of the strait and then went about again, this time without risk of getting in stays. Twice more they had to tack before a second dark butt of land loomed ahead. Lindhoved, thought Mr Fitton, in whose mind all thoughts of Anne Brennier had been replaced by a steady mental picture of the Swedish chart with the convoy moving tortuously between its submerged shoals. He was able to calculate times and distances and so keep an adequate check on the Danish skipper at the wheel, whose monosyllabic grunts, relayed by Erikson in English, initiated a series of very short tacks. This was the narrow passage between the shoals off Lindhoved and the Lillegrund bank. It was passed safely, and only just in time. On the reach to the north-east beyond it the faint wind became fitful and suddenly fell away altogether. The sails hung limply. The nine ships lay motionless on a sea as smooth as black marble.

Svane, a burly dark figure behind the wheel, took his hands from the spokes and spread them wide. Mr Fitton had not so far given the Dane any hint of his proposed destination.

"Ask him how far to Sonderby Klint," he said to Erikson.

The reply confirmed his own calculation—seven miles. The middle watch was almost at an end.

"Pass the word for Mr Sholto. And then request Mr Honeyburn to come on deck."

If they were still here in the fairway of the Little Belt when daylight came their chances of concealment were gone. Even at four in the morning, with so much light coming from the hidden moon, some small vessel might set forth from Assens to head up or down the strait; a passing fisherman might not at once realise the meaning of the fleet of eight ships and a 12-gun warship, but he was sure to report what he had seen and in twenty-four hours the narrows at Fredericia would be barred. It might be—for all he knew—the convoy's good fortune that it had fallen dead calm, virtually immobilising any Danish night sailers. But every minute they delayed here increased the risk of discovery.

The bos'n came trotting aft from the shadows of the foredeck.

"Mr Sholto, I'll have the watch below turned up. Hands to take in all sail. Jolly-boat's crew stand by."

"Aye aye, sir."

Honeyburn's saluting arm swung in the half-darkness as the bos'n ran for'ard.

"I'm sorry to rouse you before your time, Mr Honeyburn. We're becalmed and I'm going to tow. You'll please to see to the launching of the jolly-boat, with a towing-line to the bitts. Then stand by for'ard to relay steering orders to the boat."

"Aye—"

107

"Wait. And station a hand with the lead ready for sounding. Peters is a good leadsman."

Mr Fitton turned without waiting for the lieutenant's acknowledgement and went to the after rail. *Cracker* had revolved under some faint influence of air or water and her next astern, *Dragon*, was visible on the beam a cable's length away. His deep-voiced shout reached her easily through the windless night.

"*Dragon* ahoy! We're going to tow. Take in sail, launch boats. Pass the word down the line." He went to the wheel. "You heard that, Erikson—tell Svane what's happening. You'll take the word from him when he wants course altered, and hail Mr Honeyburn who'll be up in the bows—port, starboard, or steady."

"Aye aye, sir. By'r leave, sir, that looks like fog yonder."

The gun-brig was still slowly turning on her axis and Mr Fitton had to glance at the binnacle before he could locate the direction, nor'-nor'-east, in which he would be heading. There was certainly a discernible belt of paler grey lying across the surface, though it was impossible to estimate how far away. If it was fog, its convenience as a hiding-place might just balance the increased danger of running aground below Sonderby Klint.

The hollow deck thrummed to the ordered rush of feet and dark figures raced up the shrouds. The jolly-boat, swayed up from its chocks, splashed down on the water overside a moment after the last fold of canvas was furled on the yard. Sholto climbed down to the sternsheets at Mr Fitton's order, the tow-line was passed outboard to lead over the bows, and the oarsmen gave way, directed by the bos'n with the aid of *Cracker*'s only portable compass. Apart from a little Dutch *pram* which was of no use at all for towing, the gun-brig boasted only the jolly-boat. The first tug as the line came taut appeared to produce no movement at all in the larger vessel; but a second hardly perceptible jerk, and a third, set her turning, very slowly and then faster, until she pointed once more on her course. Svane, his frowning face dimly illuminated by the binnacle lamp, corrected her spin with a flick of the wheel and she began to creep through the water, so sluggishly that no tremor of movement could be felt in the planking under Mr Fitton's feet. He had divided his attention between his own deck and the sounds and movements astern of *Cracker*, where *Dragon* and the Swedish ships had been carrying out the same evolutions, and was relieved to note *Dragon*'s longboat a pistol-shot away putting the first strain on the tow-line. It was going to be hard work for the oarsmen in all nine of the boats. To some extent the lesser size and burden of the gun-brig, compared with the laden merchant ships, would be counter-balanced by the fewer oars she could pull in the jolly-boat; but a two-hour pull at the least would have to be faced. If they entered fog the rearmost ships could easily lose touch. In that case their skippers could probably be trusted to work a way inshore with lead and compass.

"Port!" yelled Erikson in response to a mutter from Svane, and Honeyburn's high-pitched voice echoed him from for'ard. "Steady!" And again the order was repeated.

Despite Sholto's compass-work the jolly-boat could still move crabwise under the strain of the towing-line and draw *Cracker*'s bows off the strict course. However, with no wind or tide or current to influence her she was safe enough for the moment, still out in the fairway with ten fathoms under her keel. It would do no harm to check that—or to stop the growing buzz of conversation on deck.

"Watch below, dismiss! Pass the word for Mr Trapp. He's to bring log and glass aft here."

With Honeyburn fully occupied in the bows and Sholto in charge of the boat, the gun-brig's deck officers were in short supply; it was a defect he had felt when he had first taken command, with the result that the carpenter found himself doing, on occasion, rather more than his strict duty.

"Mr Honeyburn! A cast of the lead, if you please." Honeyburn, sometimes remiss, had carried out his orders this time. It was Peters's booming voice that called after a pause.

"Deep nine!"

They could be passing over the slightly shallower ground shown on the chart, with less than six miles to go. Two figures were coming aft, one short and skinny, the other short and fat: Mr Trapp, and one of the hands—the Dutchman Kloos, Mr Fitton thought. He could see nothing of their faces because the faint radiance from the hidden moon had suddenly dimmed. *Cracker* had entered the mist.

"Reporting, sir, has per horder," began Mr Trapp, "I 'ave 'ere the log—"

"Mr Honeyburn! Start the lead and keep it going.—I beg your pardon, Mr Trapp," added Mr Fitton courteously.

"Aye aye, sir. I 'ave 'ere", the carpenter resumed, "the log and the glarss, sir. Also Kloos, sir, for to 'old the reel."

"Very well. You'd better stand right up to the rail or the line will foul it."

Mr Fitton took the sand-glass and stood close to Svane where the light of the binnacle lamp gave just sufficient illumination for his purpose.

"Now!" he said sharply, reversing the sand-glass as he spoke.

Trapp instantly dropped the log-ship over the quarter. It was a wooden slab so attached to the log-line that it floated vertically and resisted being pulled through the water, so the line started to run out from the reel Kloos held above his head with both hands. Mr Fitton watched the trickle of sand into the lower glass.

"Stop!"

Trapp nipped the log-line between his fingers and felt along it as Kloos hauled the dripping slack inboard. The second knot in the line was still on the reel, but only a turn or two from where he was gripping it.

"A trifle under two knots, sir—a trifle under," said Mr Trapp.

That was as good a speed as he could have expected, reflected Mr Fitton; but it meant three hours before they reached the proposed anchorage.

"Thank you, Mr Trapp," he said dismissively.

But the carpenter had something yet to say. " 'Aving but just come on deck, sir," he pronounced, "I feels in my bones—in my bones, sir, a change o' weather."

Mr Fitton waited without impatience. He had come to realise, through repeated experience, that Mr Trapp's bones were right about the weather nine times out of ten.

"East backing north we've 'ad," continued Mr Trapp, "north dropping dead calm we've 'ad. So what I say, sir, what I say is, westerly backing south—*and* freshening, *and* freshening, soon's it gets up. And that, sir, that will be around th'last dog-watch if not afore."

Mark my words was implicit in his tone. Mr Fitton thanked him again and dismissed the two of them. As they went for'ard the tenuous grey veil of mist closed behind them. It was as if the gun-brig was crawling along beneath the surface of a sea without weight or substance.

While the log reading was being taken he had been aware of the leadsman's shouts. "Deep nine" was still the sounding. *Dragon*'s towing longboat was invisible astern now, but the creak of oars in rowlocks and the objurgations of the helmsman could still be heard. Whether the other seven ships were in close line astern it was impossible to tell, and if the fog persisted he wouldn't know where they were until the anchorage was reached. The damp chill of the vapour sent a shiver down his spine and he began to walk, ten paces into the fog, ten paces back in the fog, considering the interfluent problems of rate, distance, time, and Trapp's weather forecast, with their probable incidence upon the success or failure of the convoy's passage through the Little Belt. The gun-brig held her slow course satisfactorily; the intermittent chant of the leadsman changed to "By the mark ten" for twenty minutes or so and then reverted to a nine-fathom sounding. The noises from *Dragon*'s longboat faded and renewed as the distance altered. A misty orange halo hung above the binnacle lamp, just lighting Svane's beetle-browed face. Mr Fitton, noting this as he paced up and down, noted also that the glow from the lamp had paled and that the faint light that suffused the fog had lost its hint of gold and taken on a colder hue. The moon had set and daybreak was at hand. He had turned aft in his walk when a small compact shape appeared beside his path.

"I hope I may come on deck, sir?" said Anne Brennier as he came to a sudden halt.

Mr Fitton knew that he should have sent her below again at once. It was on the tip of his tongue (or so he thought) to do so. Instead he lifted his cocked hat.

"Of course, madame. You've had some sleep, I trust?"

After all, this was his watch below; Honeyburn was officially in charge of the deck.

"The shouts woke me, a long time ago." She shivered. "It is cold, this fog. I interrupted your walk—if you will give me your arm we can continue it together."

It was ordinary courtesy for a gentleman to arm a lady as they walked, but Anne's hand resting lightly on his forearm, her shoulder touching his and her warmth and perfume close at his side, wrought so strongly upon Mr Fitton that he found it impossible to say a word. They took three turns up and down in silence. Then Svane made one of his rare demands for the course to be straightened and the subsequent interchange of

112

shouts between Erikson and the invisible Honeyburn seemed to break the spell.

"Morning is almost here," he said. "We should anchor before long and then Band shall serve breakfast for you and your father."

"Thank you, sir." There was laughter in her voice. "But pray don't think I came on deck to beg for my breakfast. It was curiosity brought me here, not hunger. Where are we going?"

Mr Fitton glanced down at her. The growing light was just strong enough to reveal her features framed in the fur-rimmed hood of her cloak, and the wave of affection that swept over him surprised him into an audible gulp which he hastily turned into a cough.

"I want to get the convoy close inshore behind the Toro Bank and anchor there," he told her. "We shall lie there until dusk tonight."

"Yes. You must creep through the Little Belt by night to avoid discovery—I understand that." Anne skipped into step as they wheeled in a turn. "What I don't understand is why you're so—pray forgive me—so vastly foolish as to bring your convoy this way instead of through the Sound."

It was too much to expect that he should not explain his seeming foolishness. He told her, as they walked, the reasons for his doings of the past four days, and under her adroit questions the story—no short one in itself—expanded into an outline of Mr Fitton's past career. For him at least time passed unnoticed. The mist filled with grey daylight and Erikson dowsed the binnacle lamp. Up for'ard, Mr Honeyburn had the leadsman relieved. Mr Fitton was not so infatuated that he failed to observe these things; he saw, too, that Baron La Haye had come on deck wearing a green cloak and a round fur cap and was standing by the rail amidships. Another thing he noticed, and had he not been so absorbed in his companion it might have made him thoughtful: Svane's sullen glance was often directed at the two who paced so amicably up and down together arm-in-arm. But the undoubted sincerity of Anne's interest in him was too enthralling to leave his finer senses free to detect danger.

Mr Honeyburn was the herald of a more immediate danger. The leadsman's monotonous chant ceased at his cry of "Still!" and he came bounding aft to interrupt his commanding officer's idyll with a confused gesture that combined a salute with a bow to Madame Brennier.

"Oars and voices, sir," he announced, hoarsely and cryptically. "I mean—I think there's some craft approaching, sir, on the port bow."

Mr Fitton heard the sounds as he ceased speaking. That was a small vessel, probably a fishing craft, pulling with her sweeps. He disengaged his arm quickly.

"Your pardon, madame." He sprang to Erikson's side. "I want you to shout as loudly and as much like a Dane as you can, Erikson. Get over to the port rail. Say this. 'Sheer off—merchant ships towing—keep clear or you'll collide.'"

Erikson obeyed, his jump to the port rail a reflex of the urgency in Mr Fitton's voice. His own voice was a powerful one and he yelled the warning vehemently. On the last word a fretwork of dark lines crept spider-like out of the greyness to port, changing its outline as the men at the sweep oars hurriedly altered course. A few words of Danish were shouted from the small vessel and as Erikson replied she completed her turn and began to fade into the mist again.

Mr Fitton had hardly glanced at the Danish craft. He was standing directly behind Svane at the wheel and could clap a hand over the man's mouth if he opened it to shout; but La Haye was at the port rail amidships, gazing into the fog, and Anne Brennier, on the starboard side of the quarterdeck, was watching her father intently. If one of his prisoners chose to raise the alarm and apprise the departing vessel that here was a British warship with a convoy bound for England that would be the end of his mission. He remembered that the parole he had extracted from La Haye and his daughter had been an undertaking not to attract the attention of people on shore; vessels encountered in the Little Belt had not been mentioned. For some thirty seconds the four—Mr Fitton, Svane, Anne Brennier and the Baron—stood motionless as stone figures, while the fog slowly swallowed the Danish fishing-vessel.

Whether because he considered himself bound by his parole or because he was apprehensive of the consequences, La Haye made no sound. Anne, presumably, had been waiting on her father's lead. In any case their chance was gone. Erikson came across to report.

"They gave us warning for warning, sir—the coast's a mile ahead an' we're heading straight for it."

Very likely the fishing-boat had been hugging the coast, following the channel that encircled the Toro Bank. It was a merciful chance that had brought her in from the port side of his course, missing the jolly-boat and *Dragon*'s longboat—and a piece of quick thinking on the part of Honeyburn.

"You did well to silence the leadsman when you did, Mr Honeyburn," he said. "Go for'ard again, if you please, but don't start the lead until I give the word."

It was quite light enough now to see Honeyburn's pleased expression.

"I'll have two hands on lookout in the bows," he added. "All hands are to keep absolute silence and the leadsman can call his soundings just so loud that you can hear them."

This fog would blanket all noise, but it was quite possible that there were other fishing-craft not far away. A mile from the coast; that meant that he must alter course due north. He passed that order through Erikson to Svane and then followed Honeyburn for'ard to shout it through the lightening mist to

Sholto and to set the lead going. The Baron, he noticed, had gone below. In the past few minutes of urgent thought and action he had completely forgotten Anne, and when he came aft again to the quarterdeck she was gone.

3

With his leather soles slipping on wet rock, Mr Fitton hauled himself up the steep flank of the coastal hills. The mist that hung all about him was dazzling white and gaining in brightness as he climbed. Still in the radiant cloud, he gained a stony crest that rose on his left hand and, turning upward along it, emerged suddenly into clear sunlight. A sea of white vapour stretched away on every hand under a pale blue sky, and a hundred yards away the rounded crest culminated in a rocky knob that reared like the head of a sea-monster raised above the cloud-waves. He clambered to its top and sat down, telescope in hand, to get his breath. It was six bells in the forenoon watch.

Three hours had passed since the abrupt shallowing of the water had warned that *Cracker* was either close in to the shore or running into a shoal. She had anchored at once, in three fathoms, and when *Dragon* loomed out of the mist a few minutes later it had been possible to hail her and see that she let go her anchor in time. With the remainder of the convoy it had not been so simple. The fog, still so dense that no loom of land was discernible, made it impossible to use signals and only by prolonged and noisy shouting had three of the Swedish ships been prevented from running aground. Old Reuterholm, cannily sounding his way, had *Ahund Jakob* riding to her anchor well clear of the shoal water before any other warning reached him. *Anjala* and *Iduna* had gone hard aground and had to spend much time and trouble kedging-off. Of the remaining vessel, Ebbeson's *Blanzeflor*, there was no sign. This much Mr Fitton had ascertained as soon as the jolly-boat was alongside the gun-brig and her weary crew replaced by fresh hands. Leaving Honeyburn to set an anchor watch and supervise the prisoners' breakfast, he had himself pulled due north from *Cracker* into the fog. Three minutes across the shoaling water he came to a shore of big stones with the loom of coastal heights beyond. With this reassurance that the convoy had reached its intended anchorage and not some offshoot shoal of the Toro Bank he could turn his attention to the state of his flock, groping his way from ship to ship to count his charges like a careful shepherd. The search for the missing *Blanzeflor* proving fruitless, he had once more headed for the shore, this time to land and climb the declivity behind the beach with the boat-compass in one pocket and his glass in the other.

Resting in the faint warmth of October sunshine on his rocky watch-tower, he found no use for telescope or compass. There could be no doubt that the little summit was Sonderby Klint, marked on the Swedish chart as 150 feet above the sea, for no other crest broke the rolling white cloud-sea in any direction; this was the highest point of land for many miles round. Wreaths and curls of white cloud were rising from the cottonwool surface of the fog here and there and he was suddenly conscious of the drift of cold air on his cheek—from west of north, it came. This ghost of a breeze might or might not be the forerunner of Trapp's shift of wind through west to south, but at least it should move the fog.

Even though there was nothing to see but cloud and sky, it was delightful to come out from the enclosing gloom of the sea-fog into light and space and the warmth of hazy sunlight. Yet Mr Fitton found himself seeking to recapture those precious minutes in the damp half-darkness when Anne's arm had been linked in his and the friendly warmth of her body close to him. He was already fully resolved that one day he

117

would ask her to marry him, though the time for that was not yet. If the La Hayes were a family of distinction, as was to be presumed, the Fittons could match them; and as for his present poverty and low professional rank—well, it was at least probable that both would be amended soon after he reached England. Until then, though, he must be careful to restrain his feelings and ensure that his behaviour conformed to what would be expected of a junior naval officer bringing home a captured nobleman and his daughter. If their Lord-ships of the Admiralty so much as suspected a breach of proper conduct—

Here his thoughts reverted from the future to the present. His meditations had not prevented him from watching the slow stirrings of the cloud around him and now his eye fell on a thin vertical line that had emerged from the shifting mass of white. A church steeple; it was less than five miles away to northward and must be the church at Assens. He took a bearing with the compass—precisely nor'-nor'-west—and made a mental note to check it with the chart. The fog was breaking up with surprising rapidity, rifts and wide holes appearing in it simultaneously with the rising and shredding-away of vapour. On the west, the seaward side, he could now look down through a widening rift to the shore and the jolly-boat lying off with the oarsmen resting on their oars. The mist parted still farther and *Cracker* came into view. The boat lying alongside her he recognised as *Dragon*'s longboat, and even without the glass he could identify the people on her deck. Honeyburn was for'ard in the bows directing a party of hands in some adjustment of the anchor-cable. There were three persons on the quarterdeck—Anne at the port rail looking up towards the crest where he was sitting, her father and the master of the *Dragon* walking up and down on the starboard side in close conversation. He saw Clewes halt his companion, apparently to make some important point which he emphasised with earnest gestures. But his interest was in Anne, and he could not forbear to wave his hand in the hope that she would see him. She raised an arm in reply and presumably uttered an exclamation, for the two on the other side of the deck turned and stepped hastily apart; a movement curiously suggestive (thought Mr Fitton idly) of two schoolboys caught plotting truancy. But now the mists were opening everywhere, vanishing as if the light breeze that rippled the ever-widening stretches of sea was the invisible wand of a magician. The seven merchant ships were revealed at anchor in an uneven row, and—to his great relief—the eighth ship, *Blanzeflor*, came in sight anchored half-a-mile down the coast to eastward. Less than a mile out beyond *Cracker* was a patch of discoloured water which must mark the shallowest part of the Toro Bank, and beyond that the dwindling vapours allowed a sight of the Jutland shore seven miles away. Mr Fitton used the compass to take a bearing of the Toro shallows and then turned his attention to the landward side of his observation post.

At once he crouched and clambered down below the skyline on the east flank. The whole landscape lay clear before him. An undulating terrain of woods and fields and uncultivated heath, a patchwork of dark greens and golds and autumn russet, stretched away to the horizon, and to northward the cluster of red rooftops that was Assens perched on the shore of the winding sound that led to the entrance of the Fredericia narrows. An unfenced road, little more than a cart-track, threaded its way from Assens to pass within a mile of his position on the hilltop, and a wagon loaded with bales of hay was moving on the road. It was this that had prompted Mr Fitton to make himself less conspicuous.

From a couch on low-growing berry plants he focused his glass on Assens. It was a good glass by John Dollond and shortened the five miles to something under one. Though

Assens was a very small place it appeared to be walled and he could make out something that looked like a miniature harbour; for small craft only, that would be, for the deep and narrow channel of the Baago sound by which the convoy would pass Assens was a mile out from the coast with shoal water between. From here the gleaming waterway looked wide and safe between its converging shores, but over the greater part of it the depth was only two or three fathoms and often less, as the chart showed. Onward in the north were the twistings of the Fredericia narrows, his final and most dangerous obstacle; but they were sixteen straight miles away and beyond his present horizon. An odd flurry of movement among the red-tiled roofs caught his eye as he took a last look at Assens; it was a moment or two before he identified it as the flapping wings of the storks that nested there.

Before he descended to the waiting boat he scanned the broad seaways to westward. There was no path or other sign that anyone ever came up to the Sonderby crest which effectively concealed the convoy's anchorage from the landward side, so the danger of discovery was greater from seaward. There were two sails in sight far over towards the Jutland coast, a schooner and a smaller vessel. Whether heading south into the Baltic or making westward for a mainland port such as Aaben at the head of its fjord, any sailing craft would keep to the deep water six miles out from the Toro Bank. Here as in the Marstal Bugt his chief risk was the fishing-smacks who might decide to try their luck among the channels. His own luck, reflected Mr Fitton, had so far been remarkable—or else his present course was approved by that Tutelary Genius which the Stoic philosophy assigned to each individual. In either case he had no choice but to hold on as he was going.

A north-westerly breeze, very light but steady, ruffled the surface as the jolly-boat took him back to the gun-brig.

Dragon's boat was still alongside, and it was Clewes who greeted him—waving aside the indignant Honeyburn—when he climbed on board. Neither Anne nor her father were on deck.

"Been waiting for you, Fitton," said Clewes with spurious heartiness. "Lucky I had your pal the Baron to entertain me. What Monsieur La Haye don't know about fishing and hunting ain't worth knowing—we'd a rare deal of talk, I can tell you."

It occurred to Mr Fitton that the merchant captain was in something of a hurry to explain his conversation with La Haye; also that it was odd that a man like the Baron should deign to walk and talk with a man like Clewes. At the time, however, it seemed no more than odd.

"I wasn't aware that you spoke French, Mr Clewes," he said stiffly.

"Danish," Clewes said quickly. "Danish I can manage better than bloody Frog lingo. But I came aboard, Fitton, to tell you we want a conference—all ship's captains, aboard *Dragon*."

Mr Fitton's brows drew together. " 'We'?"

"No need to get in a bloody huff, man. Birger and Reuterholm think as I do. I suppose you intend to hold the convoy here all day and sail at dusk?"

"I intend to take the wind into account, Mr Clewes."

"Oh." Clewes was taken aback. "Well, that's it. The wind's backing and it's bound to freshen. To get out from behind this damned shoal we've got to make a sou'-westerly course, and if it backs to sou'-west—"

"I know all this, Mr Clewes, thank you," said Mr Fitton coldly. "There'll be no necessity for a conference if you'll be good enough to pass my message to the Swedish ships. They are to have all ready for getting under way quickly—sails on a split yarn if they like. We'll sail when and if the wind backs to west-nor'-west, and at my order. That'll be flag signal before dusk, two lights at my masthead if it's after dusk. Is that clear?"

"It's going to have us close-hauled between shoals but it'll do," Clewes conceded. "You don't fancy making a run for it, clear past Fredericia, if the wind steadies southerly?"

"I don't. We can't avoid passing within easy range of the fort's guns so we'll do it by night. The risk by day is too great."

As he spoke Mr Fitton was inhospitably edging his visitor towards the rail; he had only one bottle of Madeira left and he wasn't going to waste it on Mr Clewes.

"Risk?" grumbled Clewes. "What's more risky than what we're doing now? And how d'ye know we haven't been seen and reported already? I'd lay evens they'll have their bloody boom across at Fredericia when we get there."

"You know they have a boom there?" Mr Fitton asked quickly.

"That's the story in Stockholm. Baulks of timber on a nineteen-inch cable, they say. The Danes would have one ready for blocking the Sound as well, but the Swedes won't allow it." Clewes, finding himself at the quarterdeck rail, turned to climb over. "By the bye, that's a beddable wench you've aboard here," he added over his shoulder. "Pity she don't seem at all biddable."

He climbed down into his longboat. Mr Fitton watched the boat shove off from *Cracker*'s side and then faced Mr Honeyburn, who plainly had something to communicate.

"*Blanzeflor* came up under topsails five minutes ago, sir," said Honeyburn. "I don't think you observed her. She's anchoring between *Dalarna* and *Frithiof*."

"Thank you, Mr Honeyburn."

"And—and Baron La Haye and Madame Brennier have lunched, sir, in my—in Madame Brennier's cabin." The lieutenant hesitated. "The Baron made a request which I was asked to pass on to you. He asks that he and Madame Brennier may take their meals together in privacy, in that same cabin."

It was a request that couldn't very well be refused; so there would be no repetition of that pleasant supper *à quatre*. Mr Fitton frowned.

"The Baron made this request after he'd been talking with Mr Clewes?"

"He did. But—good gracious!" Honeyburn paused, staring. "You don't think Clewes persuaded him to make it?"

"No reason why he should, that I can see. But never mind that. I believe this is your watch below, Mr Honeyburn?"

"No, sir—it's yours," said Honeyburn firmly. "Shorty—that is to say, Band—is waiting to serve a meal for you, after which I beg leave to suggest 'Elysian quiet, without toil or strife'—a phrase of Mr Wordsworth's."

"But—"

"You've had no rest or food since midnight. I've had four hours' sleep and two meals. Be advised by me, sir."

Mr Fitton allowed himself to be advised. Stipulating that he should be called at once if the wind backed to within a point of west-nor'-west, he went below. It was mere common sense, with the most hazardous section of the Little Belt approaching, to eat and sleep while he had the chance. Mr Fitton's bones were not expert meteorologists like Mr Trapp's; but he felt in them that there was trouble ahead of him.

SIX

Anne

I

"Fais honte, madame, à pleurer!"

The words, spoken as it seemed a great distance away, drifted in the half-consciousness of Mr Fitton's waking mind. He raised himself on one elbow, fully awake. The cabin was almost dark, and the faint red glow that illuminated it from the little stern window gave him an instant of uneasiness until he realised that it was not the reflection of fire but the last light of a stormy sunset. The gun-brig was making little short pitches as she jerked at her anchor-cable and from overhead came the steady thrumming of a moderate breeze in her rigging.

A murmur of voices sounded from the cabin next door but now they were subdued and words were indistinguishable. He had been sleeping with his head only a few inches from the intervening bulkhead and what he had heard was Baron La Haye angrily telling his daughter that she should be ashamed to weep—he was sure it had been no dream. Why was Anne weeping, and why ought she to be ashamed of it? Another woman in her situation might weep in self-pity, but he had come to think that Anne Brennier—

A knock at the cabin door ended his speculations and heralded the entrance of a dark figure and a smell of coffee.

" 'Ere we are, sir." said Hezekiah Band's voice. "Coffee, pipin' 'ot, nigh on eight bells, Mr 'Oneyburn's compliments and wind's a point north of west-nor'-west, sir."

Mr Fitton thanked him and groped for his jacket.

"*Dragon*'s 'ailing us, sir," added Band as he left the cabin. "Seems anxious-like to get under way."

That would be Clewes's idea. The man seemed to be incapable of weighing relative risks. Mr Fitton found the small metal case he was looking for, a new "wheel" tinder-box, and proceeded to light his cabin lamp with it. You spun the cogged wheel with your thumb and it struck sparks from a flint, and with luck the tinder—partly-charred linen—took fire. This time it ignited at the second spin of the wheel. He sipped the coffee, scalding and sweet, by lamplight and pulled on jacket and shoes. Clewes was a fool. To avoid the shoals north of the Toro the convoy had to make a five-mile reach south-west before it could head north into the first of the Little Belt narrows, and that reach would take it right into the shipping fairway; it was simple prudence to delay entering the fairway until darkness gave some chance of progressing without being seen.

Mr Fitton hurried on deck and received Honeyburn's report. The Sonderby heights stood in black silhouette against the darkening eastern sky but to westward the lurid glow of an angry sunset lingered, glinting on the small whitecaps that broke the furrowed surface of the sea.

"I'll have the anchor hove short, Mr Honeyburn, if you please," he said, and turned to the bos'n who was ready by the flag-locker. "Make 'all ships get under way', Mr Sholto."

There was still daylight enough for flag signals to be seen. Svane was already grasping the spokes of the wheel with Erikson ready beside him (for some reason the Danish skipper had elected to come on deck barefooted) and the hands stood waiting at the fore and main shrouds.

"Cable up and down!" yelled Honeyburn from the bows.

Mr Fitton glanced over the quarter and saw the flutter of canvas from the yards of *Dragon* and her next astern. His powerful voice, flung against the stiff breeze, set the capstan pawls clanking, the canvas falling and flapping from the yards, the men at the sheets hauling and belaying. *Cracker* paid off on the starboard tack and was brought close to the wind as she gathered way. In her wake followed the eight merchant ships at varying intervals, all carrying main and topsails like their leader; Mr Fitton left his topgallant sails furled since he was not concerned with speed and might even have to reduce sail to make his arrival at the proposed anchorage coincide with the first light of day.

Before turning in that afternoon he had made a close study of the Swedish chart (not for the first or the second time) and had confirmed that his distance to sail was a little more than fifteen sea-miles. The long narrow inlet called the Gamborg Fjord, diverging east from the main channel at the very entrance of the Fredericia narrows, seemed the best place— indeed, the only place—for the convoy to lurk at anchor during the daylight hours of tomorrow; and tomorrow evening he would emerge to creep through the last six miles of the Little Belt, those sharp and constricted bends that led to the exit channel under the guns of Fredericia fort. The passage of the Baago sound would be the main hazard of the coming night, but compared with that northern strait it held little danger. Narrow though it was, with a quarter-mile width in more than one place, it ran dead straight between the hidden shoals for five miles and then widened into the miniature inland sea called Bredningen. The tricky point was halfway up the sound, where the shoals on the east side, close to Assens, projected into the fairway as a two-fathom bank. If this wind continued to back south of west he would have it astern for that passage; another instance of the good fortune that had so far attended him, for it meant that the making of dangerous leeway could be avoided. But if it also strengthened, the convoy would have to take in sail. No seaman in his senses would go bowling along at eight knots, by night, between those shoals. In fact, though Svane seemed to be trustworthy enough, it might be advisable to sound his way through. As for the pilotage into the Gamborg Fjord, he would if necessary heave-to until first light so as to get his bearings from the shores.

"Sir!" Erikson spoke from beside the helm. "Svane here, he reckons we're making too far to south'd."

Close-hauled as they were, the ships would be making a fair amount of leeway in that direction. But at this speed they must already have left the middle ground of the Toro Bank astern, and the two miles of outer shoal were marked on the chart at five fathoms. He decided to trust the chart.

"Keep her as she goes.—Mr Honeyburn," he added to the lieutenant, who had come aft, "I'll have a cast of the log. Please to pass the word for Mr Trapp."

Certainly the wind was freshening. *Cracker*, heeling well over to port despite her low sails, was foaming along towards the last red bar of sunset with her convoy now following in tolerable line-ahead. Odd to think that they were heading almost directly away from Assens, a place they would pass at a mile's distance in a few hours' time. To clear the long jut of the Nordlige Lillegrund shoal the course had to make an acute angle, doubling back from halfway across the broad fairway to the entrance of the Baago sound.

Mr Trapp strutted aft with the log gear and an assistant hand, the glass was turned and the log streamed. Six-and-a-half knots. Assens should be abeam about midnight. He mentioned that estimate to Honeyburn, who had been supervising the lighting and placing of the stern lantern.

"There's some kind of harbour at Assens," he added, "but

I don't think anything bigger than a smack or one of their shallow-draught galliots could get in or out over the shoals. This Little Belt's no place for seagoing ships."

"No, sir. Let's hope——" Honeyburn's voice ended suddenly in something between a choke and a splutter.

"Are you feeling all right, Mr Honeyburn?" inquired Mr Fitton sharply.

"Y-yes, sir. It's just that—well, I was going to say—"

"Out with it, man."

"I was going to say, sir, let's hope we don't find the Little Belt too tight for us—I beg your pardon, sir."

It was now so dark that Mr Fitton's grin was invisible. "H'm," he said thoughtfully. "I think perhaps you need some rest, Mr Honeyburn. It's your watch below."

Honeyburn hastily checked another fit of spluttering. "With your leave, sir, I'd prefer to stay on deck. I—er—find this night sailing mildly exhilarating."

"So I perceive. Very well, then. I'll thank you to go for'ard and send a hand to the foremast head—Carrick has good night-sight."

"Aye aye, sir."

There was a sound resembling a smothered splutter as Honeyburn stalked away; it was not often that he made a joke.

Mr Fitton bent over the lighted binnacle for a look at the compass, nodded at the intent Svane, and began his pacing up and down the weather side. With a steady breeze and no need to alter course for an hour he could free his thoughts from the convoy and its position on the chart. He could think about the future—and about Anne.

He had not spoken with Anne all this day. He had only caught a glimpse of her once, from the crest of Sonderby Klint, and as he recalled the mental picture it seemed to him that in the gesture she had made, the upraised arm, there had been something of appeal, almost (he thought) of despair. And then, he remembered, she had turned her head quickly, looking over her shoulder to where her father and Clewes—that oddly-assorted couple—were talking together on the other side of the quarterdeck. The two brief movements conjoined hinted vaguely that Anne was perplexed or in trouble; but he could not imagine any cogent reason for it. In any case, she must be aware that he was at her service, ready to amend her troubles as far as lay in his power. At the after end of his quarterdeck walk he could discern the glow of light from the crack of Honeyburn's cabin door; Anne and her father were in the cabin—the Baron had not yet left it to go to his quarters amidships—and if she had any need of his help she had only to step out on deck.

The thought brought home forcibly to Mr Fitton the urgency of his own desire to be near Anne, to see and hear and touch her. For a second, pausing in his walk, he nearly yielded to the impulse to present himself in the cabin; there were plenty of pretexts for doing so and after all this was his ship. Then he dismissed the idea and resumed his steady pacing. The Baron had evidently decided to hold aloof from his captors as far as possible and persuaded his daughter to do the same, a decision that was easily understandable in the circumstances—and even more understandable, he realised with a thrill of elation, if the Baron suspected that Anne was allowing herself to become attracted to the commander of an enemy vessel. Would she, a woman mature and free-willed, yield to his persuasions? He thought she would. It was clear that she was closely attached to her father, had followed his fortunes from France to the Danish court; father and daughter must have formed alliance since Anne's childhood. So her present behaviour was in obedience to her father's instructions. It would be discourteous to force himself upon them when his company was distasteful to La Haye and embarrassing to Anne.

E

A rustle from the leach of the main topsail and a grunted sentence from Svane brought him across to the helm.

"The wind's still backing, sir," said Erikson. "He can't hold this course."

Mr Fitton held his watch to the light of the binnacle and estimated the distance sailed. They were not yet at the point where he proposed to alter course, and a little extra southing would do no harm considering the time he had in hand.

"Sail her full and bye," he said.

"Full and bye, sir."

Erikson repeated the order to Svane, who eased the spokes of the wheel, and *Cracker* bore slightly away to sail more freely. Honeyburn was standing by the lee rail, but Mr Fitton was in no mood for conversation tonight; he resumed his pacing on the weather side.

Astern, beyond the tilted black silhouettes of the convoy ships, the night sky held the pale radiance of a rising moon, its light already silvering the clouds that drifted across the vault of stars. A windy sky. As if to emphasise the conclusion, a thin spatter of spray came over the rail on Honeyburn's side and splashed on the deck. The wind was strengthening, from west or even a little south of it now. After the alteration of course it would be as well to make for the Baago entrance under topsails only. As he turned aft on his walk Mr Fitton noticed that *Dragon* was again not keeping proper station; Clewes's vessel had been allowed to get to leeward of the line as had happened before. Well, good station-keeping mustn't be expected of merchant ships and in any case there was deep water on every hand for five miles round at present. It would be about midnight or a little earlier when the exceedingly narrow Baago sound would demand a stricter follow-my-leader for the avoidance of trouble.

Dragon's erratic sailing brought to mind her captain's visit to the gun-brig that afternoon. It could be coincidence that

La Haye's request that he and Anne should be left in privacy had followed that visit; probably it was, since there was reason enough for that request without looking further for it, while there seemed no possible reason for Clewes to suggest it. Clewes had had a sufficient excuse for his visit—the suggestion, allegedly supported by Birger and Reuterholm, that the convoy should sail before dusk. But the man must have known that *Cracker*'s commander would not be on board. The jolly-boat, heading for the shore, had passed within half-a-cable's length of *Dragon* and despite the fog she and her occupants must have been observed by those in the merchant ship. And there was the curious circumstance—or was it so curious?—that the Baron La Haye and Clewes had engaged in what appeared to be an amicable conversation. What could a French aristocrat, a trusted ambassador of the Emperor, have in common with a man of Clewes's stamp?

Mr Fitton, aware that he had conceived a strong personal dislike for Clewes, told himself that he was prejudiced. La Haye might feel animosity towards the English naval officer who had kidnapped him and yet tolerate the company of a merchant captain; that conversation could have been about hunting and fishing after all. He was making mysteries where there were none. All the same, he could not rid himself of the feeling that there was here something unexplained, or ignore the queer tingle in his bones that hinted for the second time that day that there was trouble in store for him.

2

The moon was the beginning of Mr Fitton's trouble. It was perhaps a fortuitous beginning, for (as he was later to perceive) the trouble would have been precipitated by other means if he had not brought it on his own moonstruck head. As it was, he managed to ensure that he was helpless to prevent its first impact.

At a little after two bells of the first watch Mr Fitton gave the order to go about on the new course. *Cracker* turned plunging into the wind, the hands hauling on main and topsail sheets and braces, and swung on through threequarters of a circle to bring the wind on her port quarter.

"Steer nor'west by north," he told Erikson.

Transmitted to Svane at the wheel, this order brought a loud "*Nei, nei!*" and an emphatic shake of the head from the Danish skipper. Erikson interpreted his explanation.

"He says we're not far enough west for that course, sir—it'll take us across a corner of the North Lillegrund shoal. A three-mile run due north, he says, and then the course you gave."

Mr Fitton called to Honeyburn to take charge of the deck and went below to look at the chart, for which he had to light the cabin lamp. Svane's contention was correct, or could be so. A careful check with pencil and ruler, taken in conjunction with his dead-reckoning estimate of position, showed that the course he had proposed would take him very close to the shoal if not actually across its corner; the course advocated by the Dane, though longer, would make sure of avoiding any possible danger. This discovery removed the last lingering doubt of Svane's trustworthiness, for had he steered the course that was ordered and the convoy or part of it had grounded on the shoal he could not have been blamed for it. Mr Fitton returned on deck.

"Course due north, Erikson," he said. "And ask Svane if he's made this passage by night before."

The skipper made a longer speech than usual in reply to the question.

"Says he's passed the Baago sound a thousand times, sir," Erikson reported. "Seems he was born in some place called Assens, hereabouts."

"But by night?"

"Three times, he says, sir—and all three nights a deal less clear than this un."

Svane's bearded face, dimly lit by the binnacle lamp, was scowlingly intent on the compass-card as he steadied the gun-brig on her course due north. He muttered a sentence or two in a contemptuous tone; Erikson translated.

"Telling you not to worry or bother with the chart, sir. Because he knows the Baago sound like his ma's garden at Assens."

Mr Fitton nodded and went to the after-rail. Below him *Cracker*'s foaming wake streamed astern, snowy white in the clear moonlight, to spread and fade on the tossing black waves. Beyond it the ships of the convoy were making the 270-degree turn one after the other, *Dragon* as usual swerving too far out to port. The wind had blown the night sky clear, and silver light flashed from the racing wave-crests and transmuted the sails from jet to ivory as they turned. The strong westerly was more than a stiff breeze now. It had indeed backed a little beyond west, blowing from just abaft the beam, and its breath on his cheek no longer held the chill hint of an Arctic autumn but was fresh and exhilarating instead. Before its steady thrust the gun-brig slipped along under her two courses of canvas like a pleasure yacht of the Cumberland Fleet which Mr Fitton had once seen racing on the Thames. It was a glorious night for sailing. Exhilaration mounted within him as it had been wont to do in his early days at sea, and—as then—he felt the need to communicate it. Honeyburn was still on deck, having punctiliously transferred himself to the starboard side when *Cracker* went about. Evidently he too was stimulated by wind and starlight for his cheerful humming was audible above the shrill chanty of the breeze. Mr Fitton crossed to him down the slant of the spray-wet deck.

133

"A beautiful night, Mr Honeyburn," he said, falling into step at his lieutenant's side.

" 'Waters on a starry night' ", said Honeyburn, " 'are beautiful and fair.' Mr Wordsworth's line, sir."

"And a true one. But—'beautiful, and fair'? Isn't Mr Wordsworth laying out his sheet anchor as well as his best bower?"

"It's what's called poetic licence," Honeyburn said defensively. "He has to have his rhyme. You wouldn't blame a man for fitting a relieving-tackle on the for'ard side of a gun as well as on the after-side, now would you, sir? Or—"

"No, no—of course not," said Mr Fitton hastily. " 'Beautiful and fair'. Make it so. I only hope no hardy Dane decides it's a fine night for sailing through the Baago sound."

"No sail reported from the masthead so far. By the bye, Weldon's up there now, sir. I took the liberty of relieving Carrick."

Mr Fitton spent a moment in silent self-reproof. This was his watch and it had been his duty to relieve the masthead lookout. If he could forget the care of his men he could no longer be the efficient sea-officer he once had been—or it might be that concern with his personal affairs was running foul of his duty to his ship.

"Thank you, Mr Honeyburn," he said. "Now as to yourself. In an hour or less we should be able to make a landfall, the moon being as bright as it is. That'll be Aaro island at the entrance to the Baago narrows. I shall shorten sail to topsails then and I'd like you on deck, though strictly speaking you're not on watch until midnight."

"Good gracious, sir, I'm no stickler! You have only to—"

"I'm sure I have. I'm asking you now to go below and get some supper and a little rest. You won't have another chance before daybreak. Don't hurry yourself, but when you come on deck oblige me by bringing up my boat-cloak."

Honeyburn performed his windmill salute and departed. Alone on the quarterdeck except for Erikson and Svane at the helm, Mr Fitton resumed his pacing by the weather rail.

The prickings of conscience that had assailed him in the matter of the masthead lookout were soon dispersed by the magic of the night. The steady rush through dark waters aflash with silver light, the mingled voices of wind and sea unceasing yet ever varying, the leap and sway of the deck under his feet—these things thrilled him as they had not done for many a year. He felt a score of years dropping from him as he paced. The dark curve of the main course overhead cast its shifting shadow across the planking for'ard of the quarterdeck and his walk took him from moonlight to shadow and back, a trifling circumstance that gave him disproportionate pleasure; as indeed did everything about this brief hour of heightened sensibility. It dawned upon him that he was experiencing again the increased delight in all around him that comes to a young man in love, that all that was needed to perfect this changed existence was the presence of Anne Brennier beside him sharing that delight.

Mr Fitton stopped his pacing and halted by the mainmast shrouds where he could stare up at the moon and abandon himself to thinking of Anne. Only for a passing moment did he marvel that at forty-six, a man whose only mistresses had long been the ships he commanded, he should feel the strong urgings of passion. Not even for a moment did the warning exhortations of Epictetus cross his mind. The fantasies he conjured up with the light of the moon streaming down on his face had more to do with Diana than with the Stoics. He pictured Anne and himself in some unidentifiable paradise under just such a moon as this, with the understanding that had so swiftly begun between them now completed in the fullness of love; his arms closing round her yielding body, her parted lips expectant—

135

He heard nothing of Anne's swift approach across the deck. He looked down, still foolishly bemused, and there she was close to him, a part of his dream. He caught her to him and kissed her.

For a long time afterwards he was to remember how for one short moment her lips responded and her body pressed against his. Then she was straining back from him, beating her hands against his chest and jerking out broken phrases.

"No—you must not—you don't understand. I came to warn—"

"Madame!"

The harsh interruption came from the head of the after hatchway. Mr Fitton, letting his arms fall to his sides, saw La Haye standing there motionless; saw, too, Svane and Erikson watching him from the helm, and beyond them Honeyburn in a posture of arrested motion with a boat-cloak over his arm. The last moonlit traces of his vision shredded away on the wind.

"Madame!" rasped the Baron a second time, commandingly.

Anne took two steps away from Mr Fitton and halted. She turned towards him, putting out a hand in an uncertain gesture, and he heard the catch of her breath like the ghost of a sob. Then she turned away again and went to her father. He took her arm and they descended the steps to the cabin. Mr Fitton saw the glow of light from the opened door vanish as it closed behind them.

"Your—ah—boat-cloak, sir," said Honeyburn, coming up to him.

Mr Fitton took it from him absently. His glance went past Honeyburn to the wheel, where Erikson and Svane still had their heads turned towards him.

"Pay attention to your course, there!" he roared, so fiercely that the lieutenant jumped back from him; then in a quieter tone, "Thank you, Mr Honeyburn. You've supped, I presume?"

"Y-yes, sir."

"What do you make of the weather, pray?"

Behind the screen of expressionless voice and face he was recovering self-possession.

"Weather, sir?" Honeyburn was unused to being consulted on such a matter. "Well—the wind's certainly backed another half-point since I went below. And it's still strengthening, too. I'd say—"

"Just so. If it backs farther and blows sou'westerly the sky will cloud and we'll lose this handy moonlight." Mr Fitton took out his watch and peered at the dial. "I can expect to make a landfall at any time now. Thank you, Mr Honeyburn."

He made the last words dismissive. He had talked himself back into the reasonable world of ships and the sea and got the moonshine out of his head; he needed to be alone for a few minutes for a cool consideration of what had passed. As Honeyburn crossed to his own side of the quarterdeck he recommenced his pacing by the weather rail.

Accepting that he had behaved like a fool, what were the results? His foolish behaviour had after all been a precipitation before its time of an avowal he had intended to delay for a week or two; Anne, he felt sure, had not been deeply offended by it, though she had reason to reproach him for not choosing a more private situation. His heart leaped as he recalled her answering lips. With La Haye it was another matter. His dignity, his pride of family, had doubtless been outraged. But however closely he and Anne were bound by the ties of family and affection Madame Brennier was her own mistress where affairs of the heart were concerned. She was free to give her hand where she wished. He frowned as he remembered the few disjointed words she had uttered, then nodded to himself as he saw, or thought he saw, their meaning. In another and more

137

E*

immediate sense she was not free at all, for she and her father were equally prisoners of an enemy power; Anne could not be free to do anything while her father was deprived of his freedom. It was of this, no doubt, that she had intended to warn him.

In the sum of it, then, he had done no irretrievable damage by his lapse, as far as Anne and the Baron were concerned. More serious was his ill-conduct as a naval officer in command. He was considering this, with increasing realisation of its dangers, when he saw the brief glow from the opening and closing of the cabin door and the Baron crossed the deck to him.

"Monsieur Fitton. I have to speak vis you," said La Haye in laborious English. "*Est-ce que c'est possible*—I speak more better in my own tongue."

"*S'il vous plaît, Monsieur le Baron.*"

"*Bien.* Let us walk away a little," continued the Baron in French. "I prefer not to be overheard."

His tone was cold and precise. They went a few paces for'ard, out of earshot of Honeyburn and the men at the helm. La Haye began without preamble.

"After what has just occurred, Monsieur Fitton, it must be obvious to you that I and Madame Brennier can no longer remain on board this ship."

Mr Fitton frowned. "I offer my most humble apologies for what occurred, Monsieur le Baron. But I fear you will have to remain."

"I believe you to be a gentleman, monsieur. Our situation— my daughter's situation—is now intolerable here."

Mr Fitton would have liked to ask if Anne thought it so, but decided to refrain.

"My duty requires me to hold you as prisoners on board a vessel of His Majesty's Navy," he said.

"Pardon me, monsieur, but you have already failed in your

duty." La Haye shrugged his shoulders. "We are of course in your hands. But your superiors, your admiral and those lords at your Admiralty, will not look kindly on you when they learn of your behaviour. You have assaulted a lady of birth who had by chance become your prisoner. You forced lascivious embraces upon her against her will."

"That is not true," said Mr Fitton in a voice that trembled with restrained fury.

"No? Then my own eyes are at fault. Also the eyes of your lieutenant, your seaman, and the Danish skipper you hold as prisoner. I believe, Monsieur Fitton, that my eminence, even as a prisoner in England, is sufficient for my word to be taken against yours. And if it were not, I can name three witnesses."

"And Madame Brennier?" Mr Fitton could not help saying.

"She will do as I say." The Baron's voice lost some of its chilly arrogance and took on a venomous note. "The little fool may have taken a passing fancy for you. She might say a word in your defence, if she was allowed to. But nothing can alter the fact of your actions, monsieur, or the disgrace that will be your reward."

There was a short silence. Mr Fitton was attempting to assess the effect of the threatened accusation. Even if it failed— and he had to admit this was unlikely—the damage would be done. Its mere publication would be enough to end his career and bring incalculable trouble upon Anne.

"Naturally," La Haye resumed in a reflective tone, "I would dislike having to appear in such a cause at one of your English courts-martial. Moreover, it would be very distasteful to have Madame Brennier's name cited publicly, as it would have to be. I would much prefer to keep silence on the whole matter, Monsieur Fitton. And I will do so, upon my honour, on one condition."

"And that condition, Monsieur le Baron?"

"It is simply that you place us on board another ship at the first opportunity. There is an English ship in your convoy, the *Dragon*. Her captain has already offered his hospitality should I be able to persuade you to let us remove. Escape will be no less impossible for us there, monsieur."

So that was what Clewes and La Haye had been talking about. Well, there was little he could do except agree; with Anne involved, the risks of refusal were too great. Clewes would have to surrender his charges when—

"La-and ho!" screeched Weldon from the masthead. "Port bow—fine on th' bow."

Mr Fitton was slow to come out of his preoccupation and it was Honeyburn who shouted back.

"How far distant?"

"Could be three mile, or four. Hard to say in this light."

Aabo island three miles on the port bow; it was time to alter course. Mr Fitton brought his attention back to La Haye.

"Very well. I will arrange for you and Madame Brennier to be put aboard *Dragon*."

"At the first opportunity?"

"At the first opportunity, Monsieur le Baron."

La Haye turned on his heel without another word and went back to the cabin. Mr Fitton, forcing his own cares to the back of his mind, straightened his square shoulders and returned to the care of his convoy.

3

From his swaying perch on the foretops'l yard, whither he had climbed with the heavy boat-compass in his pocket, Mr Fitton easily made out the island of Aaro, a flat black bar separated from the much longer black bar of the mainland by a scarcely perceptible gap. There was a short cut to the northward through that strait between Aaro and Jutland, he knew; but though the channel was never less than seven fathoms according to the Swedish chart, it was even narrower than the Baago sound and more twisting. So Aaro must be left on the port beam with its neighbour island Baago. He took a bearing of Aaro, with some difficulty because of the necessity of holding on with one arm round the topmast. There was moonlight enough to see the compass dial, but even as he noted the bearing the needle and the lettered points became invisible. A cloud, outrider of an oncoming squadron in the south-west, had obscured the moon.

Before clambering down to the deck he noted that not only Aaro island but also the coast opposite to it was in sight, the latter just discernible as an undulant line on the rim of the eastward waters. The four miles of sea between them, where his course lay, looked safe enough to accommodate a battle-fleet at anchor. The chart knew better. There was only one safe channel through those huge hidden shoals and it was no more than 400 yards wide for much of its length.

As soon as he was down and aft by the helm he passed the results of his observations to Svane by way of Erikson.

"Aaro bears north by west. Between two and three miles by my estimate, but distance-judging isn't easy at night."

Svane nodded his satisfaction when this was translated to him and commented shortly in his own language.

"We should alter course at once, sir," Erikson interpreted. "Nor'west by north."

"Very well. Steady as you go.—Hands to shorten sail! Mr Sholto! Get the main courses in."

The men of the watch-on-deck raced up to the mainyards and in less than a minute the courses, flapping at their slackened sheets, were furled and the gaskets on.

"Bear away, quartermaster. Steer nor'-west by north. Tops'l braces, there!—Mr Honeyburn, I want a cast of the log, if you please."

Honeyburn loped away for'ard shouting for Mr Trapp. *Cracker* eased her heel to starboard now that she was under topsails alone and had the wind over her quarter, but she was still foaming along at a good rate of knots. The wind was certainly blowing more strongly. The wave-crests astern showed big white teeth as they broke—a dead white like bleached linen, for the livelier glint of moonlight was gone and overhead the thick flight of clouds covered the sky and hid the stars. The eight convoy ships were tall dark shapes with no relieving touch of lighter hue, untidily spaced as they straggled on the dog-leg course occasioned by the alteration, black rags of canvas flapping and vanishing as each vessel followed *Cracker's* lead and took in her courses.

Honeyburn, Trapp, and one of the hands came aft and proceeded to heave the log. Five knots; under topsails alone, that was fast sailing—too fast for Mr Fitton's liking. He glanced across at the helm, where Svane was stamping his bare feet to warm them. The Dane seemed confident enough. It was evident, from his behaviour when he had had a clear chance of running the whole convoy aground on the North Lillegrund shoal, that he could be trusted to steer a safe course through the Baago sound. If he was as experienced in these waters as he claimed to be there was no point in groping a way through with the lead.

Except for *Dragon*, who was indulging her customary tendency to lie too far to port, the line of ships was now straight astern of the gun-brig. It was like an arrow flying towards an invisible target—the quarter-mile width of safe water midway between Aaro and Assens coast. Mr Fitton pulled out his watch and took it to the binnacle light: twenty minutes past eleven. Midnight should find him halfway through the sound with Assens a mile away on his starboard beam, and an hour and a half after that he would be out in the central bulge of the Little Belt with four miles of deep water on either hand to play with and plenty of time to get the convoy out of the fairway and concealed in the Gamborg Fjord before daylight. One more night, less than four hours of sailing with a wind like this, and the last hazard would be passed and the clear run to the Kattegat and England awaiting him.

With that prevision of success there came to him the realisation of the risks he had taken. He had gambled on the Belt being devoid of sailing-craft by night, on the lack of observation from the shore by day, on a succession of favouring winds, and the dice had fallen well for him on every throw. Luck had stood with him on the one occasion when danger came close—the fishing-boat that had hailed them in the fog—for it was only by luck that Erikson was on deck and able to hoodwink the Danes. Fortune was indeed on his side for the making of this passage; but not, it seemed, for the progress of his love-affairs.

By now Mr Fitton was becoming accustomed to the alternation of his two pressing anxieties. He had been able to keep himself from consideration of the action forced upon him by La Haye until the convoy was safely headed for the Baago Sound. Now he could think about its implications.

It was distressing to have to send Anne away from *Cracker* and no less so to know that it was his own fault. Beyond that, however, the prospect was by no means dark. Clewes would have no choice but to hand over the two prisoners as soon as the convoy was past Sheerness; nor could La Haye object to returning into the charge of his naval captor. Mr Fitton felt reasonably certain that the Baron's word of honour was firm as adamant, and that the Baron would deem it dishonourable to use his threat of disclosure to exact any further concessions. So the roseate visions of a future of promotion and affluence with Anne Brennier to share it were in no way diminished.

Behind this satisfactory conclusion lurked an unsatisfied doubt. By La Haye's own showing Clewes had been anxious to have the prisoners on board *Dragon*; the man's inordinate vanity would sufficiently explain this, for both were persons of distinction and the fact that he had brought them from Denmark in his own ship would win Clewes some little fame among his fellows. But had it been at Clewes's suggestion that the Baron had watched for an opportunity of bringing his threat to bear? If so—and how neatly he had played into their hands!—Mr Fitton found the subtle planning, the nasty ingenuity of the plot, oddly ponderous to achieve so insignificant an end. No. It must have been the coincidence of the Baron's wish with Clewes's invitation, precipitated by his own moonlight folly, that had brought about the sorry result. He dismissed the matter from his mind, firmly resisted the inclination to wonder whether Anne was thinking of him at this moment, and brought his attention back to his course.

The whole sky was now covered by a rack of hurrying clouds, but the luminosity from the hidden moon was sufficient to show the low black hump beyond the tossing waters on the port hand: Aaro island, little more than a mile distant and broad on the beam, which meant that they were in the narrowing jaws of the unseen channel.

"Sir!" came Erikson's voice. "Wind's still backing—I reckon it's dead sou'-west now."

Mr Fitton went over to look at the compass and then peered up at the main topsail.

"Mr Sholto! Ease away on the lee braces."

Cracker had the wind so fine on her quarter that it was practically astern. It could hardly have been better for this tricky passage.

"Ask Svane if he's sure of his course," he said to Erikson. "Remind him there's a two-fathom shoal to starboard two miles ahead, off Assens."

There was impatience in the Dane's voice as he answered. He knew that shoal very well, Erikson translated, and had passed it many times without touching. Honeyburn, who had approached the wheel, spoke out of the darkness, raising his voice to top the now considerable noise of wind and sea.

"If we run aground at this rate, sir, we could lose a spar."

"Hardly that, if the Swedish chart's accurate. But the convoy ships might." Remembering something that Honeyburn should know, he drew him a few paces from the helm. "As soon as we anchor, Mr Honeyburn, I shall want the jolly-boat lowered to take Baron La Haye and Madame Brennier to *Dragon*. I've promised that they shall be transferred at the first opportunity that offers."

"Good gracious!" Honeyburn sounded shocked. "I beg your pardon, sir, but have you thought—"

"I've thought and I've decided. But I don't want to appear myself. You'll escort them on board Mr Clewes's ship."

It was the best way, he thought, to avoid possible embarrassment for himself and Anne.

"Aye aye, sir," said Honeyburn in a puzzled voice. "But—"

"I'll thank you to go for'ard, Mr Honeyburn, and see that the anchor's clear and the cable ready for veering. I don't anticipate any kedging-off but we'll be prepared for it."

When Honeyburn had gone Mr Fitton went to the after-rail for another look at his convoy. A moderate sea was getting up now and the rising wind blew a thin shower of spray into his face from the curling wave-tops. It was not so easy to make out the line of ships as it had been an hour ago but *Dragon*, close astern, was far enough out of station to port to reveal the vessel next in line. Clewes's laxity, or his helmsman's, could endanger his ship; but nothing could be done about it in these conditions. At least he could see no other vessel out of line.

As he turned to face for'ard a tiny spark of yellow light caught his eye. It was on the starboard bow, and as he peered at it across the dark white-flecked water he could see that it was on the upper edge of a black line of coast. That light was in Assens. It looked surprisingly close, but lights on shore were notoriously deceptive as to their distance away.

He watched the yellow spark move round towards the beam as *Cracker* sped on into the narrows with her train of vessels behind her. The light was nearly abeam now. Assens was more than a mile east of the channel, as he knew from the chart—yet he could have sworn that the black loom of the coast was nearer than that. Was Svane—

The dawn of suspicion came too late. He had taken one step towards the helm when the deck lurched under him and he staggered and fell. The gun-brig lifted, touched bottom again, and slid clear. A savage yell from Erikson came simultaneously with Mr Fitton's brief vision of a burly figure hurtling past him as he scrambled to his feet. He was up in time to see the burly figure dive clear over the starboard rail into the tossing sea. Even in that catastrophic instant he remembered noting casually that Svane had been barefooted at the wheel.

SEVEN

The Narrows

I

There was a prayer of Epictetus to which the youthful Michael Fitton had been much attached: "Bring on me now, O Jupiter, what difficulties thou wilt, for I have abilities by which I may acquire honour." In middle age, on that windy midnight in the Little Belt, Mr Fitton would have wished (had he thought of it) to add a postscript: "But please bring them one at a time."

For Svane's calculated steering-error and subsequent dive over the rail set in motion a whole train of mishaps following so close on each other's heels as to be accounted simultaneous. Erikson had been flung to the deck by a sweep of the Dane's arm and the helm was left temporarily unattended. Though the gun-brig had driven clear of the shoal the double check as her keel grounded had caused her to spin round to port, to be checked again almost instantly by a violent shock. Her bowsprit had encountered the starboard rail of *Dragon*, who—thanks to her usual bad station-keeping—had sheered past the outer rim of the shoal without touching and had overtaken *Cracker*. There was a jarring crack as the bowsprit-end snapped, and the gun-brig continued to turn into the wind. *Dragon* flew on into the darkness amid a chorus of shouts; a chorus which was echoed by other yells from the darkness astern of her where one after the other the Swedish ships that had followed in *Cracker*'s wake ran into the hidden bank. Spars snapped and a heavier impact suggested a damaging collision.

By now Mr Fitton was on his feet. Thirty-two years of sea experience enabled him to grasp the present and future dangers of the situation in a moment of thought and instantly to take counter-action. He sprang to the wheel and grasped the spokes ready to meet the spin of the gun-brig when her bows came up into the wind. The tremendous voice he could produce on occasions like this easily topped the clamour of wind and sea.

"For'ard there! Let go anchor!—Mr Sholto, all hands!— Get those tops'ls in, Mr Honeyburn!—Erikson, unship the stern lantern and run for'ard with it. Stand right up in the bows and shout as you wave it."

He eased the wheel against the swing of the hull and *Cracker*, her topsails aback and flapping noisily, hung in the wind. The anchor splashed overside and she began to gather sternway as the cable was veered. Overhead the cracking of the canvas ceased as it was gathered in, and the first check of her backward progress told that the fluke was biting and holding.

"Belay!—Make fast!"

A ray of light shone from behind Mr Fitton and he heard the voices of Anne and her father. Two dark masses were swooping out of the night on *Cracker*'s starboard bow and he had no time to spare for prisoner-passengers—not even for Anne.

"Go back into your cabin and stay there!" he thundered; and the ray of light vanished as the door closed again.

The dark masses were two of the Swedish vessels. No doubt they had seen the grounded ships ahead of them in time to take avoiding action, and—by good luck—had turned away to port

148

where the deep channel ran. They passed well clear of *Cracker*, warned by the waving lantern in her bows. A third ship followed, sheering closer to the gun-brig, and someone aboard her yelled interrogatively. Mr Fitton responded by roaring "Anchor!" at her and thought he heard an acknowledging shout before she flew on into the night. That made four of the convoy, at the least, who had escaped the mischief Svane had contrived. What of the other four?

There must be good holding ground here for the cable was snubbing sharply every time the gun-brig rose on the waves. That light in Assens still shone mockingly from the coast, on the port quarter now, and a bearing of it checked at intervals would enable him to judge whether the anchor was dragging; that must be done later. He left the helm and hurried for'ard, halting at a group of hands standing by the port rail amidships.

"What are you about, here?"

"Mr 'Oneyburn's order, sir." Carrick, who answered, turned from the rail; he was holding a musket. "I was to try and 'it 'im, but there wasn't a 'ope, sir. Nary a glimpse of the bastard."

Mr Fitton had found no time for consideration of Svane's action beyond accepting that the man had got clear away. His very first impression of the Dane had been that he had the build of a strong swimmer. Svane would be safe from a weapon as short-ranged and inaccurate as a musket by the time it had been brought on deck and loaded, even in daylight, and at night there was no chance of hitting him. Even so, Honeyburn could not be blamed for trying the only possible way of stopping him.

"Very well," he snapped. "Get that musket unloaded and stowed away. Is Peters here? Peters, take charge. I want the jolly-boat cleared and slung ready for lowering. Boat's crew stand by. Garroway, go aft and stay by the helm."

149

He ran on towards the bows where Erikson stood with the lantern. Honeyburn's lanky form, at the foot of the foremast, turned as he came up.

"The lookout just reported, sir. *Dragon*'s anchored two cable's lengths astern of us, the other three ships farther away. Sholto's been out on the bowsprit—"

"Thank you, Mr Honeyburn."

He strode on, to where the bos'n and Mr Trapp, eerily lit by Erikson's lantern, were conferring beside the projecting butt of the bowsprit.

"Three foot of spar fratchoored, sir," the carpenter replied to his abrupt question. "Fratchoored and a-dangling. I've two men out-along, cutting it clear. We carry no jury-spar that I knows on."

"Bobstay's gone an' topmast stay parted, sir," added the bos'n.

"I want both of them rigged on the shortened bowsprit. See what you can do."

"Aye aye, sir."

Mr Fitton climbed onto the bow rail, holding on by the forestay, and peered into the darkness. *Cracker* was pointing into the wind, her bows towards the way she had come, and the white-crested waves that had been following her in her flight north-eastward now struck her from the south-west as if they resented her stubborn opposition. Spray burst under her broken bowsprit at every wave, drawing heartfelt oaths from the two hands who clung there using axe and knife to clear away the tangle of cordage and splintered wood. Staring beyond the repeated showers, he could see white drifts of spray flying at intervals against the dark hulls of two grounded ships. They were rather less than a quarter of a mile away as far as he could judge. The ceiling of cloud that obscured the moon had grown thicker in the past hour and the dim radiance that now scarcely lightened the darkness was insufficient to let him see more than that. Of the other two ships he could see nothing, but they were almost certainly aground farther away. While *Cracker*'s lesser draught had taken her well across the shoal before she touched, the much deeper draught of the laden timber vessels had driven them onto the hidden bank as soon as they had begun to cross it. The one comfort was that these Little Belt shoals were soft shoals, sand or small stones instead of rock like the fatal underwater reefs of the Caribbean. Even so, considerable damage could be sustained by a ship driven aground by a strong following wind—which, too, would increase the difficulty of getting her off again. His next task must be to ascertain the extent of the damage to the four ships south of him.

He stepped down from the rail and as he did so the solitary spark of light ashore caught his eye. If he could see that, the folk in Assens (if any were awake) could see him. There was no point in calling attention to his position even if it had already been noted.

"Set that lantern down in the scuppers," he told Erikson. "And stand by to come with me in the jolly-boat. Mr Honeyburn, I'm going to pull round the vessels that are aground. You'll take charge here. I suggest the first thing you do should be to take a sounding overside."

"That's done, sir," said Honeyburn with satisfaction. "I used the rod as soon as we began to veer cable." He pointed to the thirty-foot sounding rod that lay in the scuppers beside the flickering lantern. "I could just find bottom with it."

Cracker must be close to the edge of the shoal, then, for the channel of the Baago Sound was eighteen fathoms along this stretch.

"That was well done, Mr Honeyburn. Now, I don't believe she's dragging but I want a bearing taken of that light ashore and checked every ten minutes while I'm away."

"Aye aye, sir. The light's in Assens, of course." Honeyburn

paused. "Svane, sir—if he gets ashore, will they attack from Assens?"

Mr Fitton had deliberately concentrated all his attention on the convoy's present emergency and left consideration of his future course until its problems had been dealt with. He found, however, that some inner corner of consciousness had been at work on the matter of Svane's escape and weighed its consequences.

"Svane has a mile or more to swim with a cross wind and rough water," he said. "He can't have got ashore yet but in my opinion he will. He's known in Assens and they'll believe what he tells them, which will include the fact that *Cracker* mounts twelve guns. According to the chart, the place has shoal water by way of an approach so it's impossible that any vessel of force should be there. They can't attack us."

"Gunboats?" suggested Honeyburn. "Or batteries?"

"In the middle of Denmark, where they'd never expect an enemy to penetrate?"

Peters materialised out of the obscurity to report the jolly-boat ready for launching. Mr Fitton gave the necessary order and turned to Honeyburn again.

"No, Mr Honeyburn. Unless they're all fools in Assens they'll send a messenger to Fredericia. That's where the guns are—and a boom they can bottle us in with while the guns finish us off."

"Dear me!" Honeyburn sounded mildly concerned. "Then we have to get to Fredericia before the messenger from Assens."

"Or before they close the strait with their boom. If we can." Mr Fitton took two paces aft and then came back again. "Relieve the masthead lookout, if you please. Send a good man aloft and tell him to keep a sharp eye on Assens. And Mr Honeyburn—have all ready for making sail, as soon as that's possible."

"Aye aye, sir."

The jolly-boat was rising and falling on the black waves that hissed alongside. He climbed outboard, gauged his time, and dropped into the sternsheets beside Erikson. A fluttering bundle fell into his lap a second before the bowman shoved off.

"Boat-cloak!" Honeyburn called from the rail.

Mr Fitton shouted his thanks. As the boat lurched away from *Cracker*'s side he turned to look back. Two figures, black against the paler darkness of the sky, stood at the quarterdeck rail apparently watching the boat. The shorter figure, he knew, was Anne Brennier. On an impulse he took off his hat and waved it above his head, hoping she would see. She raised a hand in reply. He could just make that out in the darkness, and it was a gesture he was always to remember. An instant afterwards she was gone, hurried away as it seemed by the man beside her. Mr Fitton huddled the boat-cloak round his shoulders and headed the boat into the black welter of the waves.

2

The seas raised by the sou'-wester were steep but short, and though the spray flew aft in a stinging shower each time the bows drove through a curling white crest the jolly-boat was not shipping enough water to necessitate baling. Mr Fitton was glad of his boat-cloak, and not only for its protection from a soaking. For the first time since Svane's escape he had time to consider his own folly in the matter; and in the consequent depression that assailed him it was a sort of comfort to reflect that Honeyburn at least (perhaps Anne, too) did not regard him with the contempt he was feeling for himself.

He it was who had been responsible for running the convoy ships aground. A court-martial would find as much, and with justice. He had handed over the helm of the leading vessel—his own ship—to an enemy, a prisoner, and the result had been precisely what could be expected. That was what they would say. And he had no defence, for the excuse that he had trusted Svane because he thought the man sufficiently overawed by the threat of reprisals on his master and mistress appeared ridiculously flimsy—moreover, in the event he had been proved utterly mistaken. It would be vain to plead that Svane's behaviour in warning him that the convoy was too close to the Nordlige Lillegrund shoal had been adequate ground for trusting him; it was all too obvious, now, that the Danish skipper would make sure of running aground on a shoal within swimming distance of the coast.

Mr Fitton eased the tiller to starboard, peering into the spray-wet darkness for a first sight of a grounded vessel. What should be his procedure if he found one of the Swedish ships so damaged that she could not continue the voyage?

He had been blind, of course, blinder than any bat. Svane might have been intimidated by the danger to his employers at first, but he must quickly have perceived the fraud. He had been at the helm when Madame Brennier and her captor had walked and talked together; he had heard Anne laugh. He had seen Mr Fitton take her in his arms. He could be sure that the action he was planning would not be revenged on La Haye and his daughter. Could it be, Mr Fitton wondered, that the Baron himself had ordered Svane to run the ships aground and escape to Assens? If so, he had surely broken his parole, which required him to make no attempt to attract the notice of people on shore. He would confront La Haye— But that was childish. What was done, was done. Svane, Anne, her father, were of no import in the task now confronting him, which was to save his convoy.

And here was the black bulk of a ship's hull looming ahead, with the smaller black shape of a boat tossing astern. She was laying out a kedge anchor. He headed the jolly-boat towards her side.

"Erikson, I want to know her name and whether she's damaged. You can say *Cracker* and four other vessels are anchored clear of the shoal."

Rising and falling on the wave-crests, the jolly-boat came within easy hail of the Swedish ship. Those on board were at first too busy to notice Erikson's hail but after repeated shouting an officer came to the side and replied to the interrogation.

"*Ingria*, sir," reported Erikson. "No damage that they knows of and they reckon they can kedge her off all right. Wants to know what the pilot's playing at."

"Don't answer that one. Tell her to sound nor'-west until she's in eighteen fathoms and hoist a light to the mainmast-head to show she's ready to make sail."

He would have to risk showing lights now if he hoped to get under way before dawn. The voice replying to Erikson's shout sounded querulous.

"Asking how many more times he has to run aground, sir," Erikson said.

"Did he acknowledge my order about the masthead light?"

"Yes, sir."

"Very well. Give way, all."

The jolly-boat pulled clear of *Ingria*'s side and was headed to circle round the boat laying out the anchor. Mr Fitton heard the splash of the kedge going overboard as he turned to port in search of the next ship. With luck, he reflected, *Ingria* would be anchored in the deep of the channel inside an hour.

The second grounded vessel was easy to locate. She was only half-a-cable's length from *Ingria* and from her deck came men's voices singing lustily. She had a kedge anchor out already and the hands were heaving-in on the cable to the rhythm of a

155

capstan-chanty. It was no surprise to find that this was *Ahund Jakob*, old Reuterholm's ship.

Reuterholm himself came to the side for the shouted exchange with Erikson. *Ahund Jakob*'s fore-topmast had snapped on the impact with the shoal, he said; he carried a jury-spar and could rig it when there was light enough to see.

"Tell him it must be rigged as soon as his ship's anchored in eighteen fathoms," said Mr Fitton.

The old man replied angrily. He would try to get the jury-mast rigged in the dark, but he insisted on Mr Fitton coming aboard for a talk; if he refused, Captain Reuterholm would refuse to sail. Mr Fitton promised that he would come aboard on his way back from inspecting the remaining ships, and pulled away. Two vessels in sailing trim for Fredericia, or soon to be so. All now depended on what had happened to the other two.

He found them close together, a cable's length to southward of *Ahund Jakob*. Erikson's shouts established that they were *Frithiof* and *Dalarna*, and it could be seen that *Dalarna* was afloat; but Mr Fitton had to board *Frithiof* in order to find out the state of affairs. Between Captain Birger's attempts at speaking English and Erikson's interpretation of his fluent and wrathful Swedish, the explanation took some time. Birger, it appeared, had seen his next ahead, *Ahund Jakob*, ground on the shoal and had instantly put his helm over, unfortunately turning his ship to starboard and so hitting the shoal himself. *Dalarna*, following close astern of him, had been quick to imitate the turn to starboard but not quick enough to avoid a collision. The port side of her bow had struck *Frithiof*'s starboard quarter and the planking of both ships was stove in. One effect of the collision shock had been to prevent *Dalarna* from ramming her forefoot hard into the ground, so that she was now afloat though too close to the shoal to manoeuvre under sail.

Mr Fitton managed to assuage Birger's anger without revealing the fact of Svane's escape (he had resolved to keep this from the Swedes if he could) and then had to inspect the damage to *Frithiof*'s stern planking. Birger had his carpenter working on a temporary repair; the damage was well above the waterline and would only cause serious leakage in a bad storm. He was ready to admit this and reluctantly agreed to set about kedging-off and preparing to sail. With a final reminder that *Frithiof* should sound her way into eighteen fathoms before she anchored, Mr Fitton left him and had himself put aboard *Dalarna*. Here he found his most difficult obstacle. Captain Vasa, blond-bearded and scowling, declared that the hole in her bows made it unsafe for *Dalarna* to sail until it was properly repaired; the repair his carpenter was making now would not stand a head sea. Mr Fitton made a little progress against this argument by pointing out that if the sou'-wester held for the next day or two, as was likely, *Dalarna* would be sailing most of the time on the port tack with her damaged port bow lifted higher than the starboard. When he had spent twenty minutes crouched below decks in the cable-locker with the captain and his carpenter and Erikson, examining the damaged planking by the light of a smoky lantern, he was able to suggest a method (based on extensive experience of such necessary make shifts) whereby the repair could be further strengthened. And in the end Vasa agreed to kedge his ship out into the channel and lie ready for sailing.

He had sweated in the airless cable-locker. Back in the jolly-boat with the night wind tearing at his drenched boat-cloak he was chilled to the bone. He could forget this familiar discomfort, however, when he made out a dark shape lying well to port of the course he was shaping for *Ahund Jakob*. Old Reuterholm had succeeded in kedging her off and she was at anchor in the channel. He realised with a qualm of anxiety that at least an hour had passed since he had pulled away from

Ahund Jakob. The spray blowing off the wave-crests drove at his back as he steered the jolly-boat towards the anchored ship, then slapped in his face as he brought her alongside head-to-wind.

The warmth of Captain Reuterholm's cabin was welcome. The old man said little until he had poured a glass of schnapps for the Englishman and (at Mr Fitton's gestured hint) another for Erikson. Then he spoke a single word: *"Gif."*

Mr Fitton gave. His terse report on the condition of the ships that had run aground, translated sentence by sentence, was received in silence. Only at the end of it did Reuterholm speak.

"He wants to know what you've done with the Danish pilot, sir," said Erikson.

The old Swedish captain hunched in his chair across the table had not taken his gaze from Mr Fitton. He looked like a white sea-eagle, with his snowy eyebrows and piercing blue eyes. To tell him less than the whole truth would be unwise as well as dishonest; yet if Reuterholm refused to take the only remaining chance of reaching England the rest would be certain to follow his example.

"Translate carefully, Erikson." Mr Fitton looked steadily at the captain. "Svane played us false. I was to blame for trusting him. He escaped and will be in Assens by now. They—"

"Fredericia," Reuterholm interrupted, nodding.

"Yes. They're bound to send off a messenger. He'll alert the fort there. Clewes says they have a boom for closing the strait. But alerting the gunners and rigging the boom will take time. We still have a chance—"

Again he was interrupted, this time by Reuterholm's abrupt departure from the cabin. A few seconds later his voice could be heard shouting hoarsely on deck.

"He's hailing the hands at work on the foremast," Erikson

said. "Telling 'em they've got just twenty minutes to finish rigging the jury-spar."

Mr Fitton sighed his relief. He and Erikson were on their feet and ready to go when the old man came back. He wanted to know how soon the other ships would be ready to sail and what sail Mr Fitton proposed to carry. Topsails only, Mr Fitton told him, until they were out in the wide Bredningen— and the lead going all the way. Then all plain sail. As to the ships, *Frithiof* would probably take longest to be ready, say an hour. Reuterholm made a contemptuous noise. Birger was always as slow as an old cow. He strongly advised Mr Fitton to make his two-light signal for getting under way as soon as he was back aboard *Cracker* with the jolly-boat hoisted inboard; Birger would pull his breeches up quick enough and come along.

On that they parted. In better heart than when he had left the gun-brig, Mr Fitton once more got down into the stern-sheets of his boat and turned her bows down-wind. The orange star ahead of him was at *Ingria*'s masthead—she was anchored in the fairway. Her hull was invisible in the blackness until he was almost within hail of her, for the moon had set and any fading luminosity left in the sky was obscured by low heavy clouds. This was the dark hour before dawn; he realised it with a shock. It seemed only a short time ago that Svane had dived overside.

"Give *Ingria* a hail," he said to Erikson, sheering the jolly-boat nearer. "Message for Captain Horn. Be ready to sail. Use the lead. We shall not anchor again in the Little Belt."

It was as well to have two ships at least aware of his intention to sail straight on in daylight. The rest would know it as soon as he led the way out across the Bredningen, which would be at break of day if he followed Captain Reuterholm's parting injunction. *Cracker*'s familiar shape loomed close on the starboard hand—he had almost missed her in the dark. As

159

he put the tiller to port a voice hailed loudly from her deck.

"Boat ahoy! What boat's that?"

"*Cracker!*" Erikson bellowed; that was the correct reply, indicating that the boat had *Cracker's* commanding officer in her.

Honeyburn had evidently posted deck lookouts to guard against a possible boat raid from Assens. The jolly-boat lurched round and lay tossing under the gun-brig's side. Honeyburn was at the rail as Mr Fitton climbed over with sea-water streaming from cloak and clothes.

"Any serious damage, sir?" he asked urgently.

"None that will prevent us from sailing within the hour.—Is that you, Mr Sholto? What's your report?"

"Rigging complete on th' shortened bowsprit, sir," replied the bos'n with satisfaction. "We got a ringbolt through the stem for the bobstay—"

"Very good, Mr Sholto. I want the jolly-boat hove aboard and lashed on the chocks. See to it. Mr Honeyburn, I'm going below for a change of rig."

"Sir!" Honeyburn stopped him as he turned. "Masthead hailed—he saw a sail putting out of Assens. Heading north."

"Ah. What sort of craft?"

"Impossible to say. The lookout thought it was a small cutter."

"How long ago?"

"Not more than ten minutes."

The chance was still there, then. Mr Fitton turned again to go below and again his lieutenant stopped him.

"*Dragon* sent a boat, sir, not long after you'd gone. Mr Clewes came aboard, asking what had happened. I told him about Svane, and the likelihood of delay because of the vessels grounding astern of us. I said you'd sail as soon as possible and continue throughout the day. I hope that was correct, sir?"

"Quite correct, Mr Honeyburn." Mr Fitton was not going to blame him for making the obvious deduction. "Anything else?" he added, as Honeyburn still barred his way.

"Yes, sir." Honeyburn sounded nervous. "Baron La Haye and Madame Brennier are on board *Dragon*. They went with Mr Clewes."

For a moment Mr Fitton was speechless. Anne was gone. Somehow he had been counting on seeing her first, perhaps exchanging a farewell word or only a glance.

"You took it upon yourself to do this?" he said angrily. "Without my permission?"

"No, sir." Honeyburn stood his ground. "I'd your word for this, and so had the Baron, as he told me. They were to be transferred to *Dragon* at the first opportunity."

That was true enough—and this would be the only opportunity.

"I beg your pardon, Mr Honeyburn. You were perfectly right." He stepped to leeward of the lieutenant to wring the water from his boat-cloak. "I'll return on deck in five minutes. Meanwhile, the masthead lookout is to report as soon as he can see four—no, make it three lights to south'd of us. I want the anchor hove short and a leadsman standing by, if you please."

"Aye aye, sir."

Mr Fitton went down to his cabin. Honeyburn had already removed his belongings to his own quarters and appeared to have taken with them a woollen jersey which had been placed on top of the bundle. Mr Fitton went to get it. In the other cabin the sense of Anne's presence came so strongly upon him that he stood motionless with the jersey in his hand for a good half-minute before damning himself for a fool and hastening to get out of his wet clothes. He was behaving as if he had lost Anne for ever, whereas it was only a matter of a few days before they would be reunited in England. And with that prospect to urge him on, nothing should stop him from

F

bringing the convoy safely through its last and greatest hazard.

<h1 style="text-align:center">3</h1>

"By the mark seventeen! . . . Deep eighteen!"

Monotonously the leadsman called his soundings as *Cracker* ran before the wind in the grey dawn light with her tail of ships behind her.

"Like Little Bo-Peep with her sheep," commented Honeyburn, looking aft from the quarterdeck rail.

"As far as I remember," said Mr Fitton gravely, "the young woman not only lost her sheep but also left them to come home by themselves. You'd better try another simile, Mr Honeyburn.—Port half-a-point," he added to the man at the wheel.

Honeyburn chuckled. "I'll substitute a line of Mr Wordsworth's," he said. " 'We all are with you now from shore to shore'—that's the case of our friends the Swedes and I'll wager they know it."

He was in unusually high spirits, as was his senior. Mr Fitton was cheered by the knowledge that in another half-hour or less he would be able to hoist mainsails and topgallants in addition to his topsails, and race across the open waters of the Bredningen; the fact that it would literally be a race he found not less cheering, in spite of the vital necessity of winning it. But he suspected that Honeyburn's elation was in part due to Anne's being no longer on board the gun-brig.

"Deep fourteen . . . deep fourteen," intoned the leadsman.

Two long ribbons of dark grey ran beneath the paling sky on either hand: the mainland coast to starboard, the coast of Baago island to port, each about a mile away. The grey line to port was falling back ahead, the line to starboard was curving round so that he could still see it on the bow.

"By the mark thirteen!"

The channel was shallowing as it widened. The Swedish chart, which had so far proved admirably correct, was as clear in Mr Fitton's mind as if it had been engraved there. He was almost into the mile-wide fairway that emerged into the Bredningen, where there was a minimum depth of seven fathoms. All he need do was to shape a course equidistant from the port and starboard shores, and these were every minute becoming more distinct. Even now he could make out patches of forest, low undulating hills, a marshy inlet.

"By the mark ten! . . . By the mark ten!"

"Port a full point, quartermaster," said Mr Fitton. "Mr Honeyburn, I'll have her under all plain sail, if you please."

Honeyburn strode aft shouting orders. Sholto's whistle shrilled, the hands poured up from the forehatch, canvas crackled and filled as sheets and braces were hauled. *Cracker* gathered way like a horse under the spur and flew across the white-flecked grey surface with the wind over her port quarter. Mr Fitton, with a keen eye on the starboard coastline, ordered the helm yet another point to port to conform with the westward-curving sound and so brought the wind on his beam. It was with some relief that he noticed that the breeze, though it had backed now to south-by-west, had not increased in strength; much as he needed speed, he was not anxious to run the tight bends of those narrows ten miles ahead before a wind blowing half-a-gale. Looking astern, the curve of his course had brought each ship of the convoy into view, eight three-masters foaming along under full sail.

He had sailed as soon as the masthead lights had shown that three of the grounded ships were free and ready, hailing *Dragon* and the others as he passed them and ordering them to up-anchor and follow. True to Captain Reuterholm's prediction Birger of the *Frithiof* had not allowed himself to be left behind, though he had so far been unable to make up for his late start and was last but one in the line, with a considerable gap between his ship and the next ahead. Mr Fitton was somewhat surprised to see *Dragon* astern of *Frithiof*. Doubtless Clewes's already demonstrated impatience would make him overtake and get nearer the lead when they reached the freer Bredningen waters—and then, with his glass, he might perhaps have a sight of Anne if she was on deck.

"Land ahead!" bawled the masthead lookout. "Fine on the port bow—an island, seemingly."

Brandso island, that would be. In a minute or two it was visible from the deck, a low mound barely rising above the hurrying wave-tops. It was more than one square mile in extent but its highest point must be less than two dozen feet above sea-level. Between Brandso on the west and the coast on the east there was a brief strait two miles wide, a gateway to the little inner sea of the Bredningen whose northern end narrowed into the bottle-neck entrance of the Fredericia strait. Sixteen sea-miles, little more than two hours' sailing at this speed, and the convoy would be passing the fortress of Fredericia—or failing to pass it.

"Sail-ho! Right ahead, sir—small craft."

"Whither heading?"

"South'd, sir."

So it was not the small craft that had put out from Assens, the messenger carrying the news of the convoy's coming. That, of course, was next to impossible; the messenger had forty minutes' start of him and had further increased his lead because of the necessity, for the convoy, of sounding a way out of the Baago narrows. For the third time that morning Mr Fitton tried to calculate the probabilities. Say the messenger craft had now an hour's start of him. If she was a cutter, a fore-and-aft rigged boat, she would have had the advantage over square-rigged vessels in a headwind on so narrow a course. But with this steady following breeze from astern (it would be a beam wind on the easterly reaches of those bends) he could fairly assume equality of speed. On that assumption the cutter would reach Fredericia while the convoy was still an hour short of it. That would be towards the end of the morning watch and the place would be astir. Svane would almost certainly be in the cutter. Svane could invoke the name of King Christian himself to accelerate the preparations for the convoy's reception, so the guns commanding the half-mile of water that had to be passed would undoubtedly be ready. But would the Fredericians have time to tow their boom into position across the mouth of the strait?

The sail that had been reported by the lookout caught his eye and his thoughts were interrupted. She was a big galliot, not unlike a Thames barge in appearance, and she had been tacking southward. Now she was hove-to within hailing distance on his starboard beam, looking (if a vessel could so look) as though she was staring with dropped jaw at the unexpected sight of nine tall ships speeding northward in line ahead. A questioning shout came faintly from her. Honeyburn, on the other side of the quarterdeck, took off his hat and waved it in reply. Then she was past, swiftly falling astern, and the flat green raft of Brandso island was on the port beam a mile away.

There was daylight enough to see colours, but there was little colour in sea or sky this morning. No break showed in the low grey clouds, which were thick enough to hide any sign of sunrise. The furrows between the white-crested ridges of the waves were a dark grey-green. And now Brandso slid astern and they were out in the wider Bredningen with the coasts on either hand scarcely visible from the deck.

"Mr Honeyburn! Please to send the hands to breakfast, by watches. Fifteen minutes each. Then I'll want all hands on deck."

"Aye aye, sir."

"And in half-an-hour I shall order clear for action and all guns load."

"Aye *aye*, sir!" responded Honeyburn, grinning as if he had been promised promotion.

Mr Fitton returned to his summing-up of the uncertain future. All depended on whether the Fredericia boom was in position when he reached it. He could run the gauntlet of the fortress guns with a fair chance that none of his charges would receive a crippling hit; the range was short, but the Danish gunners would be firing at targets moving across their front at seven or eight knots, and it would be a lucky shot that brought down a mast or holed a hull at waterline. But the boom—well, he had only hearsay evidence as to the boom but he must calculate as if it was fact. *Baulks of timber on a nineteen-inch cable, they say.* A nineteen-inch cable, six inches in diameter, might just possibly snap if a sizeable vessel—a fully-laden three-master—sailed into it at eight knots. Just possibly. Much more probably the ship would be dismasted, the boom left intact, and no alternative left to him but abject surrender.

He took a turn or two up and down the quarterdeck. The ships astern were keeping an admirable line, which was as it should be though a trifle disappointing. It was oddly unlike Clewes to miss the chance of these open waters, which would allow him to show off *Dragon*'s undoubtedly superior sailing qualities by pulling out of line and overtaking. There would after all be no glimpse of Anne for him. It was a passing thought, for he had a more important matter to consider.

From the deck no sail was visible on the broad grey expanse of the Bredningen and presumably none could be seen from the masthead. That was natural enough; there were no ports marked on the chart, the nearest being Kolding and Gamborg, both at the head of side fjords. Sailing traffic was likely to be sparse. He went for'ard, found Mr Trapp, and went down with him to the carpenter's cabin.

When he came on deck again Honeyburn was at the port rail with his glass to his eye.

"Masthead reported sails to port, sir," he said. "Half-a-dozen fishing craft, I'd say. You can just make 'em out from the deck."

Mr Fitton used his own glass. Beyond the cluster of sails close inshore the country looked more hilly than it had appeared farther south. The coast was less than four miles distant and he could see patches of wood and cultivation, a church spire, a cluster of red-roofed houses. As he looked these details were blotted out by a grey rain-squall.

"La-and ho! Port bow, stabb'd bow, right ahead."

The man at the masthead sounded anxious. And no wonder, thought Mr Fitton ten minutes later. Seen from the deck, the converging shores seemed to meet, sealing the northern end of the Bredningen. His glass showed him a lumpy hill on the coast lying back at the end of what seemed to be a deep and narrow bay, but his memory of the chart told him that the channel, less than a mile across, turned sharp left, westerly, at the base of that coastal hill.

"Mr Honeyburn, pass the word for the bos'n. Then have the guns of both broadsides cleared away and run out, if you please."

Honeyburn's screech as he ran for'ard set the deck in a bustle. Sholto trotted aft, his shaggy red head crowned with a ridiculous woollen cap.

"Signals, Mr Sholto. Make 'Line ahead, close order.' "

Close order, by his initial arrangement with the convoy, meant half-a-cable's length between ships. Three hundred feet was as near as he dared to bring them at this speed on the constricted course now to be sailed. As the signal flags soared to the yardarm the rumble of the gun-trucks died away along the deck and Honeyburn came aft with his flailing salute.

"Ship cleared for action, sir. Guns not loaded."

"Very good, Mr Honeyburn. All guns load, 4-pounders with ball, carronades with grape." Mr Fitton glanced astern and raised his powerful voice. "Sheets, there! Spill your wind, fore and main courses!—Well enough. Haul taut and belay."

The temporary diminution of *Cracker*'s speed had brought *Ahund Jakob*, who was next astern, within half-a-cable's length and Reuterholm in his turn was slackening the sheets of his lower sails. Ahead the dark bar of the coast was rising right across his bows. On either hand the shores were fast drawing in towards him, and the wind, funnelled by their convergence, came now and then in stronger gusts. Ten miles. Eighty minutes' sailing. There must be no mistake from now on.

"I'll take her for a spell," he said to Garroway, who was at the wheel. "Stand by to take over at my order."

Into the gut of the entrance flew the gun-brig with a squall on her tail, driving straight for the shore, half-a-mile away, below the lumpy hill. The bluff of land to port fell back and suddenly there was the channel curling away to north-westward. The wind came broad on the beam as he spun the wheel, and *Cracker* heeled sharply to starboard.

"Braces, there! Smartly!—Mr Honeyburn, I'll thank you to take charge of the deck. There's an easterly bend two miles on."

A fine drift of rain came off the line of shaly cliffs close on the port hand, chilling the left side of his face and setting the deck planking agleam with grey light. On the starboard hand he caught sight of a group of wooden huts down by the shore, boats at moorings, two or three men standing at gaze. The glimpse was gone in a second, so near were the shores and so fast was he speeding between them. The strait varied in depth between twenty-four and nine fathoms throughout its serpentine length but was nowhere less than nine fathoms. He had only to hold to its centre line—except at this point just ahead where a knob of grass, an island no bigger than a sheer-hulk, lay off the eastern coast. An easing of the wheel, a recovery, and it was past. Through the thin haze of rain he saw the shore bending across his bows again and on the starboard bow a flat headland with fifty-foot cliffs dropping from it. Galsklint—and round it the strait went in a ninety-degree bend to eastward.

"Stand by to go about, Mr Honeyburn."

Round she came with creaking yards and canvas banging, reeling over to port as the breeze whistled through her starboard shrouds. When she had steadied he spared a quick glance over his right shoulder to the convoy ships astern; until now his whole attention had been concentrated on the helm. Three of them were rounding the Klint, well spaced and following him exactly. The rest were still hidden and he could only hope that there were no stragglers. There would be no possibility of aiding a vessel that went aground on one of these bends through bad seamanship; unless she could kedge herself off, in which case she would have to run the gauntlet of the Fredericia guns by herself, she would sooner or later be boarded and captured by the Danes. *Dragon* had still been last in line when they entered the narrows. He wondered what Anne was doing at this moment, what she was thinking, whether she realised the danger to which he was going to expose her in the next hour or so.

A hail from the lookout brought his full attention back to his course. A small vessel, fore-and-aft rigged, had come into sight round the next bend, tacking against the wind and heading to cross his bows. He held on, and she flew across a pistol-shot from his shortened bowsprit, the men in her shouting unintelligibly. Mr Fitton grinned to himself; unless she was prepared to tack in and out of a line of eight fast-sailing ships she'd have to heave-to and wait for the procession to pass. As he neared the bend he felt the tension of excitement and his hands tightened on the wheel-spokes. This was the penultimate curve of the strait, the one before the last eastward turn into

169

F*

open water and safety, and when he rounded it he would come in sight of Fredericia two miles ahead. If they had gunboats there and had got them to sea in time, this was a likely place to meet them; it was for this eventuality, possible but not probable, that he had his gun-crews standing ready. The rain-squall driving over *Cracker*'s starboard quarter came astern and then over the port quarter as she foamed round the turn and headed just west of north. A steep headland, the Strib, stood out on the east shore marking the final turning-point of the narrows. Beyond it, faintly seen through the haze of rain, he could make out the opposing headland, a low bluff shaded red and grey. The red must be the tiled roofs of houses. The grey beneath, in orderly horizontals, was the stone of the fortress and its batteries.

There was no sail in sight on the intervening two miles of narrow water, so the messenger from Assens had arrived. Or was at that moment coming alongside the quay; the convoy had made such speed that the cutter's lead must have been substantially reduced. There was a chance yet.

"Take the helm, Garroway," he said. "Mr Sholto, bend on a signal ready for hoisting—'All vessels anchor'. Mr Honey-burn, your careful attention, please."

In half-a-dozen terse sentences he detailed his plan for emergency. The lieutenant's jaw dropped.

"But—good gracious, sir! If the guns over yonder—"

"You may reply at discretion if any of *Cracker*'s guns will bear. Remember, that signal is to be hoisted and the ship brought to the wind the instant I hail from the masthead. Bear up to port, Garroway—lay her bows on the steeple you see above the town up there."

With that, he sprang to the shrouds and climbed swiftly to the masthead. *Cracker* was just bringing the sharp point of the Strib headland on her beam. Straight ahead and some mile and a half distant the town of Fredericia hung on its opposing headland above the fortress walls. The Strib slid back like an opening door, revealing the narrow northern entrance of the Little Belt round the corner stretching eastward to widen beyond the Fredericia point into grey waters reaching to the horizon.

Mr Fitton's glass was at his eye the moment he had settled himself on the rocking crosstrees. It showed him, after a few seconds of search, the line of bobbing black dots or bars extending across the surface of the strait from below the fortress nearly to the southern shores under the Strib—nearly but not quite. Two large pulling-boats lay close inshore there and men were busy at the water's edge. The boom was being secured. He had lost his race by a matter of minutes only.

EIGHT

The Gauntlet

Mr Fitton's lusty bellow from the masthead brought an immediate reaction. Even as he got his feet on the ratlines he felt the violent lurch of the mast as *Cracker* came round head-to-wind with her canvas flapping deafeningly a few feet from his ears. Sholto's signal hoist had sailed up to the yardarm and the anchor-cable was roaring out through the hawsepipe before he jumped down to the deck. His first glance was to the convoy ships. *Ahund Jakob*, prompt as ever, was already going about preparatory to anchoring and he could see that the two ships astern of her were about to follow her example. Amidships in his own vessel the hands were swaying the jolly-boat off the chocks. Honeyburn came loping up to him.

"Anchor's down and seems to be holding, sir. I think I could slew the starboard 4-pounder round so as to bear—"

A dull report interrupted him, followed two seconds later by another. Both men jumped to the rail to look for the fall of shot. The short steep waves topped with whitecrests made it difficult to discern.

"I think I saw it come," Honeyburn said. "Half-a-cable short. They're 12-pounders, I'd say."

"Then that's extreme range they're firing at. Let's hope they've nothing bigger."

Thirty-two-pounders might well pitch their shot into the middle of the convoy ships, who were now anchoring untidily in a huddle close to the western shore. But to command a strait little more than half-a-mile wide 12-pounders would be more than adequate; it was likely enough that the Fredericia battery mounted fewer than six of them.

"Try and draw their fire," said Mr Fitton, "but not until I'm away. What do you do when you see my signal, Mr Honeyburn?"

"Hoist 'All ships get under way', up-anchor, and make for the jolly-boat, sir," Honeyburn gulped. "I wish you'd let me take the boat—"

"You'll also man the port broadside and blaze away at the fort as you pass. The more shot they fire at *Cracker* the less they'll have for the convoy."

Two guns banged from the fort, almost simultaneously. No splashes could be seen on the wind-whipped sea.

"I believe they've only four guns up there," said Honeyburn. "I took a good look at the quays under the fort, sir, and I couldn't see anything that looked like a gunboat."

But there were a number of small craft there. If the Danes thought to put armed boarding-parties in them they might be a danger; *Cracker*, anchored down to leeward, would be helpless to aid the convoy. It was essential to do what he had to do as quickly as possible.

"Where's Mr Trapp?" he demanded abruptly.

"'Ere am I, sir." The carpenter, in a tarpaulin coat and nursing a long oilskin-wrapped parcel, stepped forward. "Complete, as I may say, with the necessairy—"

"Boat's alongside, sir," broke in Sholto, coming up.

"Very well, Mr Sholto. Arms?"

"Cutlass each man, sir. Pair o' pistols, two muskets same bein' loaded, wrop up in oilskin, sir."

"With the necessairy tool," finished Mr Trapp, not to be cheated of his conclusion.

Mr Fitton did not hear him because he had dashed down to his cabin to get his own tarpaulin coat, which had in its pockets certain important items. A gun boomed from the fort as he came on deck again and the splash of the shot caught his eye—well short of *Frithiof*, who had anchored slightly nearer the fort than the others. They were trying to hit the convoy, then; but the range was a mile and a quarter at least and the chances of success were meagre. He looked for *Dragon* and located her on the far side of the little fleet that tossed at anchor with brailed-up sails. The low green hills above the western shore, displaying a field or two but no habitations, looked very close behind them, but the ships were a good mile and a quarter from the Fredericia fortress and *Dragon* was in rear of the rest. Anne, he told himself, was in no immediate danger. This parting glimpse of the ship that held all his hopes for the future had occupied only a second or two. He turned away, bustled Mr Trapp over the rail, and followed him down into the boat that rose and fell at the gun-brig's side.

The jolly-boat could pull three oars a side. Double-banked as she was, she was carrying six oarsmen, Mr Fitton at the helm with Trapp beside him on the stern thwart, and a hand in the bows—Hezekiah Band, Mr Fitton saw. Nine men was a full load and he would have preferred less in the steep following sea through which she now began to bucket her way; but there were those two boats at the Strib end of the boom to reckon with. If they had started to pull back to Fredericia they would no doubt try to intercept him, especially if the Danes were armed. Would boats engaged in towing out a boom carry arms? In any case, he hoped he would not have to engage in a fight at close quarters, with cutlass and pistol, in a boat whose gunwales had only about six inches of freeboard.

"Lay your backs into it, lads," he said. "Every second counts now."

The wind was not dead astern but it was helping them. The jolly-boat leaped across the wave-tops, wallowing in the green troughs between them and giving Mr Fitton some hard work at the tiller. The rain, which had slackened five minutes ago, began its thin horizontal drive again, throwing a silver veil across the grey fortress walls that loomed nearer on the port bow. A stab of orange flame came from the walls as he looked, and another. Had they seen the jolly-boat yet? There was no sign of a shot falling near him. This rain might delay discovery for a minute or two but they were bound to see him before long and guess his purpose.

Oars and wind between them were sending the boat over the water at racing speed—she must be making six knots at the very least. Twelve minutes to cover the distance, then, and seven of those had gone already. He bore against the tiller, bringing the bows a point or so to starboard; the quartering breeze was causing the boat to make leeway to port and he was steering to reach the boom at its middle point. There it would be that the long chain of rope and timber-baulks would be strained most taut by the continuous thrust of sea and wind, and there also it would be most convenient to open the gateway for his convoy.

"Boat on the stabb'd bow, sir!" yelled Band, who had half-risen in the bows as the jolly-boat climbed a wave. "Close inshore, she is."

From the next wave-crest Mr Fitton caught sight of the boat, a sizeable craft; she was a quarter of a mile away yet, pulling towards him from the shore below the Strib. The second boat he had seen from the masthead was not in sight— the shore itself was out of sight behind the racing wave-tops— but as he looked for it he saw a white column lift from the sea and sink again, and heard the loud report of the discharge.

They were firing at him now, but they'd surely stop when their own boat came nearer. For that matter, it would be a lucky shot that hit a small boat moving fast on a rough sea, even at this short range.

Band was yelling again. "I seen it, sir—the boom!"

He was pointing out on the starboard bow. Rising bent-legged in the swaying boat, Mr Fitton saw it too, the huge black baulks of timber rolling and spouting like whales, the thick cable that linked them lifting clear for a moment when the waves tossed their ends aloft. As he had expected, the boom had been forced into a great curve, and he was heading into the bight. The Danish boat was closer, perhaps three hundred yards away.

"Stand by to go about," he told the oarsmen. "Mr Trapp, make ready."

While the carpenter stripped the oilskin covering from his package Mr Fitton used one hand to free the two muskets that lay at his feet in the sternsheets. Then he rose to his feet, stooping to keep a hand on the tiller. A long black shape heaved itself on a wave-crest fifty feet ahead.

" 'Vast pulling. Port oars, one good stroke." He swung the tiller as they pulled and the jolly-boat spun round with her stern towards the boom. "Now—pull together! I want her held just clear of that baulk."

It wasn't going to be easy. The heavy log plunged and reared a few feet from the tossing stern of the boat. He'd have to rely on the judgement of the men pulling the stroke oars, and misjudgement could bring that lump of timber down on the stern to sink him.

"Now, Mr Trapp! Try three feet clear of the log."

The carpenter leaned from the stern, saw in hand. It was a strong well-kept saw, the pride of his life, and it had been set to perfection an hour ago by Mr Fitton's order. Mr Trapp looked over his shoulder, his wrinkled face piteous.

"The rust, sir!" he wailed. "It'll never recover—"

"Get at it, man!"

Mr Fitton's roar set him to work at once, but it was literally touch and go. No sooner had he set the saw edge on the straining, jumping cable than the surge of the boat, or the swing of the timber-baulk, jerked it off again.

"Boathook—quickly, Band!"

The boathook, slid across the shoulders of the oarsmen, came to Mr Fitton's hand and he rammed the spike of it against the baulk, using the pressure to balance the conflicting motions of boat and boom. Trapp, precariously teetering on the stern thwart, got his saw into action and the wet strands of hemp began to part. No knife or cutlass, however sharp, could have made such immediate inroads on the hawser.

"Look out, sir!" screeched Band from the bows.

Mr Fitton turned and saw the Danish boat a hundred yards away. He had time to note a man standing in the bows with arm outstretched and then a violent blow on his left arm all but sent him overboard. He dropped the boathook and grabbed one of the muskets. Both were fitted with Forsyth percussion-locks and he had only to cock it. The pain in his arm as he raised it to his shoulder was sharp indeed, but he took aim and pulled trigger. At the same instant the man in the Danish boat bent down—to pick up a second pistol, as it appeared. Before he could present it Mr Fitton, who had seized and cocked his second musket without waiting to see the result of his first shot, aimed and fired. The Dane's pistol flew from his outstretched hand into the sea and he toppled backwards onto the rowers behind him. The boat, now only a biscuit-toss away, slewed round off its course.

Hezekiah Band was waving a cutlass and shouting something about bastards and mincemeat. Mr Fitton told him sharply to pipe down and spoke over his shoulder without taking his eyes from the Danish boat, which had not resumed its attack.

"How is it now, Mr Trapp?"

" 'Arf through, I am," panted the carpenter. "There'll be a wallop, sir—I say a wallop, in another minute."

Every second the Danes held off made it more likely that only the one man in their boat had been armed. Mr Fitton's left arm had gone numb and was practically useless. He managed to drag a pistol from its covering, cocked it, and levelled it at the Danes, at the same time letting out a ferocious yell. There was a second boat to deal with and it was wasteful to use powder and shot if intimidation would do the trick. It did. There were at least a dozen men in the Danish boat, but the haste with which they lugged at their oars to head her away towards Fredericia showed that they were not prepared to face his pistol and Shorty Band's cutlass.

There had been no cannon-shot aimed at the jolly-boat since that first one; the gunners in the fort would be afraid of hitting their own boat or even breaking the boom. The guns were still firing, however, presumably at the anchored convoy, and in the moment of relaxation following the departure of the Danish boat Mr Fitton thought he heard *Cracker*'s 4-pounder replying. Balancing in the rearing boat, he turned to see how Mr Trapp's saw was progressing, but his glance fell first upon the second Danish boat. It had been farther east along the shore, he remembered, which explained its later arrival. Now it was visible through the fleeing tail of a grey rain-squall, three hundred yards away and pulling hard towards him across the turbulent water. A second glance confirmed his first impression—in this boat there were soldiers, green uniforms with white cross-belts. They'd have muskets and they were already within range.

"*Pull!*" yelled Trapp suddenly. "She's going—I say she's—"

The oarsmen, reacting to the urgency in his voice, pulled the jolly-boat's stern clear a second before the big hawser snapped. The saw had parted all but the last strand and the combined force of wind and sea did the rest. The nineteen-inch cable, released from tension, reared like a sea-snake and splashed aside to starboard, while the timber-baulk to port began at once to recede. The way of escape was open. It remained to bring the convoy through it.

2

Mr Fitton, who had been thrown on top of the carpenter by the forward thrust of the boat, wriggled clear but remained crouching in the sternsheets.

"Put her about!" he ordered. "Let her drift and keep two fathoms clear of that baulk." Then to Mr Trapp, "Help me— I've only one good arm. Port-fires in one pocket, tinder-box in the other."

Between them they succeeded in preparing the signal equipment. The spark caught at the third spin of the wheel. Something struck hard against the jolly-boat's side and the sound of a scattered volley followed.

"Muskets!" said Mr Trapp, unreasonably indignant. "Shooting at us, the—"

"Hold that steady!" snapped Mr Fitton. "Lower—out of the wind."

The short fuse on top of the port-fire sputtered, well alight. He got to his feet, grasping the firework by its wooden handle, and held it above his head. The red flare as it burst into flame seemed brilliant in the gloomy morning—*Cracker* could hardly fail to see it, but there was no harm in lighting the second one to make sure. He heard a single musket-shot and then distant shouting.

179

"See that, sir!" Band shouted excitedly. "Bee-autiful! Oh you lubbers, you!"

"The other port-fire, Mr Trapp. Light the fuse and hand it to me."

Only when he had the second flare burning did Mr Fitton look towards the boatload of soldiers. They were farther away than when he had first seen them and after a moment he saw why. Presumably the men had been landed to haul in and make fast the end of the boom, and their boat had been beached to eastward of the boom-end, so that they had been forced to put off on the outer side of the long floating barrier of hemp and timber. They were still on the outer side and unable to get past. The boom, parted at its centre, was sweeping back like the two wings of an opening double-door, and the southward wing, swinging slowly but relentlessly on its hinge at the shore end, had trapped the Danish boat and was carrying it back before the irresistible push of wave and wind. They would get clear in time, of course, and try to pull round its outer end, but by that time—

The crash of six guns in unison came down the wind. It was no thunderous broadside, but it was *Cracker*'s; Mr Fitton's heart bounded and for the first time he allowed himself to notice matters beyond his immediate duties and dangers. Here she came, running free, with the wind over her quarter blowing the smoke of the discharge out on her bow. The grey walls overlooking the strait jetted flame and puffs of smoke. He tossed the smouldering flares away and sat down on the stern thwart, conscious now of burning pain as he put the tiller over to bring the jolly-boat away from the drifting end of the broken boom. The gap was a good cable length wide and widening every second.

"'Vast pulling, lads. What the devil are you at, Mr Trapp?"

The carpenter, beside him, was slitting the upper part of his commander's coat sleeve with a knife.

"A hinjury, sir, did ought to be dealt with immediate," he said. "Has you know, I'm acting surgeon—"

"You can act later," said Mr Fitton impatiently. "Belay that now. It's merely grazed the bone, I fancy."

As he spoke *Cracker* fired her port broadside a second time—quick work, and a good mark to Honeyburn. She was near enough already for him to see a round hole in her fore topsail, so she hadn't got off entirely unscathed. The boat that had first attacked him was visible, close under the fortress walls. Farther away he could see the sails of the Swedish ships moving out to run for the open boom, but it was not possible to distinguish *Dragon*. He fervently hoped that Clewes would have sense enough to keep Anne and her father below decks out of harm's way; a falling spar was the likeliest danger and anxiety rose in him as he imagined what could happen to her.

Cracker came foaming up across the tossing water to pass a pistol-shot away, with Honeyburn waving his hat from the quarterdeck and then turning away to screech orders. The gun-brig went smartly about and brought up head-to-wind to give the jolly-boat a lee as Mr Fitton took her alongside. He had to accept an undignified shove-up from Trapp and a helping hand from Honeyburn in order to get himself on board. Honeyburn's long face wore a curiously apprehensive look as he confronted his commanding officer but apprehension changed swiftly to mingled alarm and concern when he perceived Mr Fitton's limp left arm and the blood that dripped to the deck from his fingers.

"Good gracious, sir, you're hurt!" he exclaimed idiotically.

Mr Fitton could not forbear to smile despite his pain. "A trifle, Mr Honeyburn. Have the jolly-boat hove aboard and lashed on the chocks, if you please."

"But the wound should be—aye aye, sir," Honeyburn finished hastily. "Shall I get under way?"

"Not until the last convoy vessel has passed us.—Well done, lads. Secure the 4-pounders, load starboard carronades."

The last words were to the men at the guns, spoken as he hurried for'ard. The danger was by no means over yet—*Cracker* was still within long cannon-shot of the fortress, and she might have to go to the aid of a disabled ship. Standing right up in the bows, he saw the three leading Swedish vessels in close company passing the fort. Cannon flashed and banged at intervals but the brief white fountains of the plunging balls showed the misses. There was surely every chance that *Dragon* would come through unscathed, carrying Anne and all his hopes for that golden future in England.

The three ships were clear: *Dalarna*, *Ingria*, and *Ahund Jakob* —he knew his flock well enough by now to recognise them. They sped past on his port side and someone in *Ahund Jakob* waved his hat, but he was too preoccupied to respond. Two other ships were passing the fort now. The gunners had only been able to reload one of their cannon but the single shot that was fired found its mark, snapping the fore-topgallant mast of the leading vessel and bringing the topgallant canvas down in a fluttering tangle across the bellying topsail. She came on with hardly diminished speed, and as she passed with her companion close astern her hands were already swarming in the rigging to clear the mess. *Anjala* and *Iduna*. Three more to come—but he could see only two sail approaching. Three guns fired from the fort one after the other and he saw the second ship yaw away from her course and regain it quickly—a hit there, probably. But he had already seen that neither of them was *Dragon*. Where was Clewes's ship?

Frithiof and *Blanzeflor* came racing past, the latter with half her stern rail shot away, but he had no eyes for them. A thin flurry of rain blew across the water, momentarily obscuring the inner strait. It passed as suddenly as it had come and showed the prospect darkly clear under the low grey clouds: the purple headland of the Strib on one hand, the fortress walls on the other, the blue undulations of the Jutland hills at the bend two miles away. The furrowed surface of the channel between was empty of craft.

"Sir!"

Honeyburn had come for'ard and was standing behind him. Mr Fitton spoke slowly and incredulously the thought in his mind. He was still staring across the water.

"*Dragon*. The Danes boarded her. They've taken her."

"No, sir," said Honeyburn; he swallowed hard. "I'm afraid—that is, it wasn't like that—in fact, sir, the—"

"Quick, man!" Mr Fitton turned on him almost savagely. "Out with it—where's *Dragon*?"

"In Fredericia harbour, sir, and if you'll allow me, sir, you need have no anxiety for—for Madame, sir," Honeyburn gabbled. "She'll be among friends and—and there you have it."

"How?"

The staccato monosyllable jerked the lieutenant into a more ordered speech.

"It was one minute before we fired the first broadside. I looked astern. All the convoy ships had weighed and were beginning to move. One ship seemed to be making northward instead of east—towards the quay, or harbour, sir. I used my glass and made her out to be *Dragon*."

"Yes?" said Mr Fitton sharply as he paused.

"She—she had two flags hoisted, sir. One was a large one, a white flag. The other was the Danish colours."

Two transient white columns rose from the waves a hundred yards away on *Cracker*'s port beam, and the double report of the guns sounded from the fort. Mr Fitton neither saw nor heard these things.

"I held my course as ordered," Honeyburn went on

hesitantly. "It seemed to me there was nothing else to be done."

"No," said Mr Fitton dully. "There was nothing else to be done."

He turned away and stared again at the stretch of empty grey water. The jut of the fortress wall hid whatever shipping might be lying at the quay. The desperate plan to beat back into the narrows and make an attempt—somehow, anyhow—to bring Anne out had passed through his mind and been instantly dismissed. It was totally without hope of success. And—he was a sea-officer with his duty to do. The cannon spoke once from the fort and the shot splashed half-a-cable's length from *Cracker*'s quarter.

"Bear away after the convoy, Mr Honeyburn, if you please," he said, turning his back on Fredericia. "Secure all guns. And pass the word for Mr Trapp to come to my cabin."

"Aye aye, sir."

Honeyburn seemed about to say something more but evidently thought better of it. He hurried aft, shouting orders. Mr Fitton walked aft more slowly and a little unsteadily. A group of his men raised a ragged cheer as he passed but checked it when they saw his face. The sudden heel of the gun-brig as she paid off on the port tack sent him lurching against the side of his cabin door and brought agonising pain to his wounded arm. The pain eased when he was sitting on his cot but mental anguish took its place with the dawning realisation of his own blindness.

Mr Trapp, entering portentously with a bucket of water and a bag of swabs and bandaging, proceeded to justify his secondary rating as ship's doctor. He had some experience but very little skill, and his efforts, which were accompanied by a wordy commentary, were not particularly gentle; but he wrested neither response nor groan from his patient. "It's my belief," he later confided to the bos'n, "as I could 've hampitated without 'im noticing." In fact, Mr Fitton's stoicism was not the result of practical philosophy but of total absence of mind.

He was reliving the immediate past, tracing all the signs that should have warned him of what was to happen. Clewes's character had been plain from their first meeting; the man himself had hinted at the potential money value of the two prisoners as soon as he was told of them—that alone should have made him suspicious. Of course Clewes's visit to the gun-brig at the anchorage below Sonderby Klint, in her commander's absence ashore, had been to make his bargain with Baron La Haye. Acting the renegade would cost Clewes no pangs of conscience but he would ask a big price for his services. No doubt the means of getting himself and Anne transferred to *Dragon* had been left to the Baron, who had merely awaited the opportunity to make his threat and his demand, an opportunity which he, Michael Fitton, had afforded him without Anne's having to act her part of decoy.

Anne—Anne had betrayed him. But what else could she do? She was an enemy, a prisoner. Her loyalties were to her father and to her country. To reveal Clewes's treachery would have been to rob her father of his chance of escape, and not only her father but herself also. For why should he assume so readily that she would have preferred a life under restraint in an alien country to the life of freedom and privilege at the Danish court? What warrant had he for so overweening an assumption? A glance, a touch of the hand—but there had been more than that. And he remembered too how he had heard the sound of her weeping in Honeyburn's cabin, and the half-sentence she had spoken in the darkness on deck: *I came to warn*—. It could well be that there had been a hard struggle between loyalty and love, that the balance had actually swayed in his favour until the Baron's arrival on deck had arrested its movement. If that was so, and every instinct urged him to believe it, there was something left after all from the wreck of his hopes. His was not a total misfortune. He had a comfort, a memory, that must be his mainstay for the rest of his life. For he knew he would never see Anne Brennier again.

"Temporairily", Mr Trapp was saying, "that will be hadequate—temporairily, sir." He gave his inexpert bandaging a pat that brought Mr Fitton back to the present with a wince. "You was fortnit, seeing as 'ow the ball passed clean through—clean through, sir, with but a graze on the hupper bone."

Mr Fitton thanked him.

"That's my diagnosius, sir," continued the carpenter. "As for the perscription, it's to rest the hinjured limb. If you'll take a spell on the cot 'ere, I'll get Mr Grattan to brew some gruel—"

"I'm going on deck." Mr Fitton got to his feet. "Sling my coat round my shoulders. You can button it at the bottom."

Grumbling protestingly, Mr Trapp adjusted the coat over the bulky wad of bandages and strappings. Mr Fitton went up the ladder and out onto the quarterdeck.

Cracker was rocking along over a grey-green sea with the seven ships of the convoy sailing in a bunch half-a-mile ahead. He looked astern, but the coasts flanking the northern narrows of the Little Belt were already below the horizon. A blurred shape rose dark above the rim of sea ahead.

"Course east by north, sir," said Honeyburn, crossing the deck to meet him. "That's Samso island, fine on the port bow."

If the wind held steady, then, they'd be out in the Kattegat by nightfall. The Skaw, the Skagerrak—and then westward across the North Sea to England; no more hazards to face except the everyday chances of wind and sea.

Honeyburn seemed to be struggling with embarrassment. His question, when it came, indicated the cause.

"How is the—the *wound*, sir?" he enquired.

He threw so much suggestive emphasis into the word that although there was a pang at Mr Fitton's heart he found himself grinning.

"Thank you, Mr Honeyburn," he said evenly. "It's mending already."

3

Old Martin, at the upstairs window of his office in the Trade Division of the Admiralty, fiddled incompetently with his Bramah penholder. The quill wouldn't fit the holder. It's this poxy Government, he told himself irritably. Get them out, and we'd have the old quill pens back again in a jiffy. A rattle of wheels and hooves on the cobbles below attracted his attention. A curricle—the Admiral's curricle—had turned into Craig's Court. Martin hurried to the inner door, put his head in to warn his superior, and was in time to open the outer door to Sir John Duckworth.

"Good morning, Martin," said the Admiral, striding past him as he bowed.

He was a not infrequent visitor of late and was evidently in a more amiable mood than usual. Martin followed him into Mr Stannard's office and stood by the door in case he was wanted.

Stannard exchanged greetings with the visitor and placed a chair for him. The Admiral laid his cocked hat on the mahogany table and nodded amiably.

"I received your note, sir, regarding the timber shipment," he said. "It may interest you to know that the material for the new spars is already on its way to the dockyards."

"You've been prompt, sir, if I may say so." Stannard sat back in his chair complacently. "I trust it has arrived in time?"

"We must hope so. I believe we may say—just in time."

"And in sufficient quantity for the needs of the Fleet?"

A slight frown appeared on the Admiral's lean face.

"Again, sir, we must hope so," he said. "It's upon that matter that I'm here this morning."

"Indeed?" Stannard swivelled his eyes to assure himself that his chief clerk was present in support. "In what respect?"

Sir John's frown deepened, but not in annoyance. "I don't wish to appear a niggler, Mr Stannard. I'm aware that my pestering, or so it would seem to you—"

"No, no," interjected Stannard unconvincingly.

"—concerning this convoy has been somewhat of a nuisance. I had my reasons."

"Of course, sir, of course. That's—"

"Permit me." The Admiral checked him with an upraised hand. "The matter was of extreme urgency, extreme urgency. Now—as I say, the shipment should prove sufficient. But I must point out, sir, that although eight shiploads were promised only seven were delivered. I'm curious to know the reason for this."

"Damme, sir, that's only natural," retorted Stannard bluffly. "I can satisfy your curiosity this instant.—Martin!"

"Sir?" The chief clerk stepped forward.

"We have a copy of the report from the commander of the convoy escort vessel—*Banger* or *Thumper*, was it?"

"Gun-brig *Cracker*, sir. I can recall the passage you require." Martin coughed and closed his eyes. " 'The boom having been cut, the convoy vessels passed through with the exception of the last in the line, merchant ship *Dragon*, which was boarded and taken by the enemy. The force under my command was insufficient to effect any reprisal. I append a note of the apparent armament of the fortress at Fredericia'—"

"That'll do, Martin." Stannard turned to the Admiral. "That explains the non-arrival of the eighth ship, I think."

Sir John grunted. "I'd want a better explanation from an officer who lost one of the ships he was escorting. However, that's the business of the Nore command." He took his hat and rose to his feet. "Thank you, Mr Stannard."

"At your service, Sir John." Stannard stood up and went with him to the door. "I hear Boney's Russian army is in full retreat from—"

"Fredericia!" ejaculated the Admiral inappropriately, halting in the doorway. "Do I understand this convoy passed Fredericia?"

"Why, so it seems, sir."

"But God damn it, that's at the north entrance of the Little Belt! The Belt's a maze of shoals and no wider than my arm—it's not a wonder he lost one ship, it's a miracle he didn't lose 'em all. This gun-brig fellow must be mad."

"At all events, he brought your timber back," Stannard said carelessly. "Good day, Sir John."

"Good day, Mr Stannard." The Admiral went out, wagging his head. "Bringing a convoy through the Little Belt! Mad as a hatter."

"No doubt he had his reasons," said Stannard, and closed the door behind him.